TRAFFICKING CHEN

Trafficking Chen

EDMOND GAGNON

Edmond Gagnon Author

Trafficking Chen

Other Books by Edmond Gagnon

<u>The Norm Strom Crime Series</u>
Rat
Bloody Friday
Torch
Finding Hope
Border City Chronicles

<u>The Abigail Brown Crime Series</u>
The Moon Mask

<u>Others</u>
All These Crooked Streets
(A Crime Anthology)
Four – A Paranormal Thriller
A Casual Traveler
(Short Travel Stories)

Website: www.edmondgagnon.com

For those taken and missing...

Prologue

Chen worked her chopsticks, deftly grabbing the fried meat and noodles, while avoiding the green peppers. The young girl shied away from most vegetables, but under the watchful eye of her mother, was expected to eat them. The chicken was a treat and welcomed addition of protein to the usually boring meal. Her father ate in silence, his gaze glued to his bowl. Chen's little brother, Guang, usually spoke loudest, but tonight the slurping of noodles replaced conversation at the dinner table.

The kitchen and dining room were combined, and barely large enough for the four-person wooden table. There were no fancy appliances, only a two-burner hot plate, a small icebox, and a rusted sink. They hoped for hot water but it rarely arrived. The painted walls had once been sunflower yellow, but years of neglect left them the patina of an over-ripe banana.

Silence wasn't unusual in the Shen household. Since Chen's parents were traditional, her father considered things like music an unnecessary extravagance. As expected in their community, he was the breadwinner and worked in a shoe factory most of his life. Like all other women, her mother tended to their home. She mended clothes for extra money to buy groceries, whenever her husband gambled away his pay. It happened more often than not.

Children were expected to find work when they came of age. Guang was too young, but Chen worked part-time at the dress shop where her mother did piece work. It was a menial job. She sorted through scraps of discarded material looking for pieces that could be re-used. She didn't mind, and imagined herself in one of their beautiful dresses, perhaps as a ballet dancer prancing across the stage.

Chen was a light eater, and thought the remaining noodles in her bowl were sufficient cover for her uneaten vegetables. She glanced around the table to see if anyone was watching. Her mother lifted her chin, trying to see what she left in the bowl. Mrs. Shen opened her mouth to speak but the door drew her attention. She gasped as two men, wearing black suits, burst into the kitchen, catching the entire family by surprise.

One thug completely filled the doorway. He was the biggest man Chen had ever seen. The smaller intruder made his presence known by scolding Mr. Shen and demanding he pay his outstanding debt. The gangster slapped her father across his face repeatedly, roughing him up in front of his family. With no money to offer, Chen's father kept his eyes to the floor and said nothing.

The vocal man continued to abuse Mr. Shen, and angrily pointed around the table at the other members of his family. Guang's eyes were as big as Oreo cookies. He slouched low in his chair, attempting to be invisible. Instinctively, Mrs. Shen reached for his hand. She broke down and cried mercy for her family.

Angered by the non-payment of debt, the smaller man grabbed Chen by the hair. Her mother began to rise from her chair, but froze when the huge man took a step toward the table. The mouthpiece continued to belittle Mr. Shen as he dragged his daughter towards the door. Chen squirmed and thrashed trying to break free.

The giant scooped her up like a sack of rice and carried her out the door.

One

Rub n' Tug

Parked in the shadows, I slouched behind the steering wheel, using one hand to balance a pair of binoculars on the bridge of my nose. The other held a portable police radio. My boss sat beside me. One rank higher, the staff sergeant was in charge of the Street Crimes Branch and there to observe the take-down for Project Rub n' Tug.

As a detective under his command, in the Break & Enter Unit, I proposed the project to my boss after receiving information from one of my confidential informants. Two brothers sold drugs from their variety store, and solicited prostitution from the massage parlor they operated next door.

Traffic was sparse and the weather was mild enough to have the car windows open. A gust of wind sent an empty pop can clanking across the pavement, causing both of us to check our mirrors. Returning my gaze to the dark void in front of me, I watched a taxi pull to the curb in front of the store. A stocky man with bushy hair exited the cab. He paused in the artificial light, like a movie star on the red carpet. Slipping on his ball cap, he entered the store.

The same man exited the business about four minutes later, and flipped his cap around backwards. He got back into the waiting taxi and left. The hat was a pre-arranged signal from my undercover operator letting us know the target was in the store, and just sold him a bag of weed. I glanced at the dashboard clock, and turned to the man in charge for formal approval. He nodded.

I keyed the radio mic and gave the command. "Go, go, go!"

It signaled simultaneous raids at three different addresses. Like football fans seeing the opening kick-off, we watched two unmarked police vans stop in front of the variety store and massage parlor. ESU (Emergency Services Unit) officers, dressed in fatigues and carrying automatic weapons, bailed out of the first van and advanced on the store's front door like a parade of giant soldier ants.

Uniformed and plain clothed officers from the Morality Unit exited the second van and entered the massage parlor. Out of my sight, but not too far away at a private residence, a third group of police officers entered the private home of the two brothers. We executed search warrants at all three locations.

Within minutes, an ESU officer poked his head out the front door of the convenience store and gave me the thumbs up. The tactical team was a precaution. Our UC had bought a gun from one the owners. We drove across the street and entered the store. The owner was in handcuffs and under arrest. Investigators searched for drugs, guns and stolen property. They repeated the process next door at the massage parlor and arrested one of the girls for solicitation.

The team at the owners' house checked in to say the brother was under arrest and a search was in progress. As the raids wrapped up, officers from the Drug Squad, Morality, and Break & Enter Units seized narcotics, stolen property, and a handgun. It was the successful conclusion of a nine-week undercover investigation.

A few days later, after we finished the essential paperwork, I was summoned to the Superintendent's office to receive payment for my CI who supplied the information that instigated Project Rub n' Tug. Digger Daniels and I had been car partners years before and patrolled the Drouillard Road area. He chose a different career path in the hope of becoming Chief of Police one day. He congratulated me on the successful operation and said he issued a divisional commendation to everyone involved.

My former partner handed me an envelope containing two hundred bucks in cash. A small reward for the risk my informant took to recover drugs and stolen property, and to get a handgun off the street. His information was also instrumental in getting a sleazy massage parlor shut down. Crime Stoppers would have paid the CI more, but tips were treated as anonymous and not sufficient grounds to obtain a search warrant.

My informant proved himself reliable in the past; I scoffed at the thin envelope. Daniels offered me an unsympathetic shrug in return. There was no use in me saying anything more, I knew that's just the way it was. The public and police brass in turn, loved it when someone helped to solve crime, but they didn't want to pay for it. They expected informants to risk their lives as if it was their civic responsibility.

When I got up to leave, my ex-partner asked me if I could stay for a minute. He sighed and said he missed the old days, working the street. One of the top five cops on the administrative totem pole, Daniels complained he spent his days putting out fires and dealing with personnel or political issues. He asked if I was happy in my current position, and if I had any aspirations of moving further up the company ladder.

Working in the same car every day, we had been more than just partners. We also socialized with friends and family in our off-duty time. Our friendship faded when Digger began his ascent up through the ranks. He mentioned his ultimate goal on more than one occasion when we worked together. How he wanted to be the big kahuna one day.

I complimented my old friend on his accomplishments thus far in his career. He said he was in a position to help me reach the next level, if I was interested. For me, that was the rank of staff sergeant, meaning a steady office job with a lot more responsibility. I was never interested in being a desk-bound ranger or moving up another rung on the ladder. Street Crimes was a good gig and I hoped they left me there for a while.

We chatted a few minutes more, tossing around the names of bad guys we'd busted and recalling some of the fun we had back in the day. It was at that moment I realized the truth in what another cop had told me. Daniels used his partners to help him climb his way to the top. It made sense when I thought about it. The only times I heard from him was when he wanted something. Maybe that's why he felt so lonely up there.

Two

Street Crimes

Anyone who truly knew me was aware I wasn't a morning person. I learned to fake it for the sake of the job, and strolled into the Street Crimes office at 7:30 am. The day shift ran eight to four. Part of my job as supervisor was to check the overnight arrests, and read the reports of residential and commercial break-ins. If follow-up was required, I assigned the cases to individual investigators on my team.

Getting in early gave me a jump on things; time to prepare the overnight stats for the boss, before he came in along with the rest of the crew. Becoming a detective in the Break and Enter Unit was a lateral transfer for me, having previously been a sergeant in the Drug Squad. The two titles were equal in rank, one being an investigative position and the other supervisory.

The Auto Squad detective was at his desk when I got in. I'm not sure why, but he started his shift an hour earlier. Probably he wanted to go home sooner. Besides the Break-in and Auto Squads, the Morality and Pawn Shop Units were included in Street Crimes. The office was considered a training ground for constables on the promotional list. Seasoned detectives helped them gain investigative experience in a variety of areas.

Street Crimes was on the third floor of police headquarters. The building was relatively new and laid out with rows of cubicles for each investigator. There were no walls separating the different units, and only our boss, the staff sergeant, had an actual office with a door. Windows along the north side of the room offered partial views of downtown and Windsor's waterfront.

Reading the overnight occurrences, I saw we had a man in custody for breaking into a downtown bar overnight. I read the arrest report and forwarded the case file to Constable King. He was due in the office at any time. There were eight other break-ins reported, about the daily average for the City of Windsor. I read over each occurrence, looking for patterns and picking out points of interest for the summary sheet.

It was a quick reference list for everyone in the office to use, and held on a clipboard near the large wall maps showing all the break-ins and vehicle thefts for the current and past months. Co-op students pinned each event on the maps, with different colors for day or nighttime, and residential or commercial occurrences. It was a good visual aid for tracking problem areas in the city.

My boss, Staff Sergeant Brian Gamble, was next to arrive in the office, followed by one of the morality cops and my two investigators. The office crew was usually punctual, with the exception of my so-called partner, Shorty Fortuna. King and Gelinas got to work on the custody I'd assigned them. Shorty slinked in ten minutes late, hoping to go unnoticed.

Fortuna and I shared a team of five investigators. Another crew worked the afternoon shift, opposite to us. We all had alternating days off, covering the day and night shifts. My previous partner, before Shorty, hadn't been much better. He ran the Police Pipe Band and when he wasn't away playing somewhere, he was busy taking care of band business.

After settling in, the boss made his way down the aisle with a notebook in hand. He checked in with the Auto Squad first to get the number of stolen and recovered vehicles. My desk was his next stop. I told him about the custody and gave him the overnight count so he could pass it up the food chain. About a half hour later the Inspector came for those same stats so he could present them at the morning meeting in the Chief's office. It was a game of numbers, and when the stats were higher than normal the brass wanted to know what was being done to correct the problem. It was reactive policing at its best.

There was no magic wand we could wave to solve crime. It was up to my staff sergeant, which really meant it was up to detectives like me, to come up with ideas on how to reduce the number of occurrences, and close the active cases. That's why it was important to pay attention to patterns, and the known criminals actively involved in break-ins and stealing cars.

One investigator was assigned to the Pawnshop Unit, a job I had worked when I was a constable. It entailed monitoring items pawned or sold, and matching them with stolen property from break-ins. When I worked the one-man unit, I implemented a data entry system. Descriptions and serial numbers of all items, taken by pawnshops, were forwarded to the police. The information was entered into our computers and any hits were followed up by visiting the pawnshop, and seizing the stolen property.

Some criminals take bigger risks for greater rewards. They break into businesses, like corner stores, where cigarettes and lottery tickets can earn them serious cash. Many commercial properties are alarmed and more visible from busy streets, making them targets with a higher degree of difficulty. Things like surveillance, special tools, and lookouts come into play, requiring a more select group of criminals. Many of those individuals are repeat offenders.

There are also doorknockers. These thieves have no imagination, and simply break into private homes when no one answers the door, assuming the occupants are out. There are exceptions. Semi-professional dirt bags surveil and target certain houses they believe have cash and expensive jewelry. In my experience, such accomplished criminals are more rare than common.

I was almost finished reading, sorting, assigning, and filing the active break and enter reports, when Gelinas told me she had a court appearance, and would be tied up most of the day. She said King was putting the Crown brief together, but they hadn't interviewed the custody yet. It had to happen before he went for arraignment, and I told her I'd take care of it.

My phone rang. It was my youngest brother, Willy. He wondered if I might be able to stop in on my way home from work. He had something to show me and didn't want to discuss it on the phone. My brother wasn't the only person who thought all the police station phone calls were monitored and recorded. They weren't. We didn't even have call display at the time.

Having worked non-stop since getting in, I was hungry and thought about food. At the other end of the office at the Auto Squad desk, Jim West slipped on his holster and badge, a sign he was heading to Tim Horton's for his morning coffee break. I waved to catch his attention and told my brother I'd stop by later. Before I could return the handset to the receiver, another line rang.

"Toasted multi-grain bagel with cream cheese and bacon?" Asked West.

"And a Diet Pepsi." I replied.

He waved and I fielded the phone call. It was the cell control officer wanting to know when he could send our custody to court. I told him to hang on to our guy, and we'd be down shortly to interview him. I sensed someone staring at me and found the co-op student standing beside my desk with a bewildered look on his face. Mornings were always the same. The world demanded immediate attention, and I was forced to wake the hell up.

Three

Giving It Up

Constable Michael King went to the cellblock to fetch our prisoner. I told him I'd set up the interview room and meet him there. My pager went off while I was testing the recording machines. There was a phone in the monitor room so I returned the call. It was one of my confidential informants, telling me he had good drug information.

Joey had given me a lot of reliable info that led to some big arrests when I was in the Drug Squad, but he knew I transferred to B & E. To be polite, I listened while he caught me up. He complained the narc I set him up with wasn't getting back to him, and didn't act on his information. He was whining.

Across the hall, King and the prisoner got off the elevator. I pointed them to the empty interview room. Two other detectives and their catch of the day occupied the adjacent one. On the monitor beside the phone, I heard them grilling the guy about a stabbing that occurred the night before.

After scribbling down the details supplied by my CI, I joined King and company in the interview room. Getting right down to business, he made the introductions.

"Mr. Sartori, this is Detective Strom and I'm Constable King."

He explained to the thief his constitutional rights and the reason for his arrest, and then asked him to repeat his full name, date of birth and address, for the record. I took the empty seat and kept quiet. It was acceptable to do interviews solo, but protocol was to question in pairs. In my experience, a second set of eyes and ears paid off on many occasions.

King was a capable cop and interviewer. I'd seen him in action several times. Getting an incarcerated stranger to open up or confess was an art form in itself, and something I had mixed success with as an investigator. I knew a few detectives who were masters at it, but even they could be thrown off their game when the first word out of a criminal's mouth was 'lawyer'.

The constable zipped through the formalities and got down to the reason the accused was there. He'd broken into a downtown bar, stolen a bunch of booze, and was caught by responding patrol officers while he fled the scene. It was a matter of luck for the bar owner, who lived in an apartment upstairs, and heard the intruder.

Upon mention of his capture, Sartori put his head down and clammed up. He had not asked for a lawyer, and answered all the unimportant questions, but that's as far as he seemed willing to go. Like you see on television cop shows, everyone arrested by the police is given the opportunity to answer to their charges. They have the right to legal counsel, but they can waive that right and talk or confess if they wish.

King changed tactics and tried using leverage; Sartori's criminal record, time he'd spent in jail, and how he was a scourge to society. Nothing got a rise out of him. Out of ammunition, my investigator turned to me; my cue to step in. King had done nothing wrong. Sometimes they talked and other times they told you to go fuck yourself. It wasn't an exact science but I knew from personal experience most people liked to talk. The trick was to figure out what they would talk about. I ignored the accused and turned my attention to King.

"Did you watch the ball game last night? I think the Tigers have a shot at the playoffs this year."

My question caught both the constable and our guest off guard. King furled his brow and stared back, not sure if I was talking to him. Sartori appraised me but remained silent. My partner caught on and played along.

"I saw the first seven innings, but fell asleep on the couch."

"You a Tiger fan?" I asked Sartori.

The accused straightened a bit in his seat and shook his head, but he didn't answer.

"You better not say Blue Jays...they might be Canadian but they haven't done shit in years...same as their hockey team...the Dead Leafs."

Sometimes, if you babble on long enough, you pique their interest or they answer just to shut you up. I let my last comment hang for a few seconds.

Sartori answered, "Yankees...they seem to be the only ones who can beat Boston, don't think the Tigers will come close to them."

The ice was broken. Afraid my lack of knowledge of professional baseball would show through, I fell back on my own experience as a youth.

"You play?"

"Not no more, the kid put an end to that."

"How old?"

"Three...like to get him into T-ball but can't afford it. And my old lady has another one in the oven."

That was the screw I needed to tighten; family was usually a weak spot. Sartori hunched forward with his elbows on his knees, leaning into the conversation. He was engaged and I reciprocated by doing the same, leaving only a few feet between us. I spoke softly but directly.

"So that's why you did the B & E...you need the quid to support your family?"

His head bobbed only slightly, not enough for an affirmative response.

"It's okay man, I understand...you've got bills to pay. You're not working?"

"My back is fucked up, I'm a roofer. Tryin' to get disability."

His eyes glazed over and I knew he wanted to talk but it had to be on his terms.

"Listen, we got you red-handed on this B & E, but I know you don't want to admit it...maybe you're afraid you'll do more time if you confess. They took your fingerprints when they brought you in, right?"

He nodded in affirmation.

"Now we've got your prints on file, and you'll have to give a DNA sample too."

Sartori scrunched his face while considering it. King sat quietly and listened.

"Let me tell you how it works. Your prints and DNA go into a database and they get compared to all the evidence we've collected at other break-ins. We'll be taking a close look at the ones downtown, in the area where you were caught."

He stared at his feet. I could almost hear the wheels turning in his head.

"Think about that. You and I both know that last night's break-in wasn't the first and only place you hit. We'll be examining any fingerprints or DNA left behind at the other bars...things like blood or hairs or even sweat. We already know how you jimmied the back doors or windows the same every time. We compare tool marks too...just like on CSI."

He snapped to attention like a deer in the forest hearing a twig break.

"You gonna try and pin all those other B & Es on me?"

He looked scared and pissed off at the same time. I reached out and placed a calming hand on his shoulder.

"Not quite. What I'd like is for us to help each other out."

"I already told ya, I ain't copping to last night. I'll take my chances in court."

"I understand that. How would you feel about admitting to some of the other one's you did if I promised you wouldn't be charged for them, even if we do match your prints or DNA?"

He stared at me for a couple seconds, and then fell back into the chair as if he was pushed. Sartori blinked and flicked his eyes all over the room, in search of a response.

"How...why would you do that?"

"It's simple math, really. We may be able to charge you with some of those other B & E's, but then again, we might not. Either way, for me, I get to close the files and make myself look good to my boss and the bean counters. And for you, if you admit to them now, I can guarantee you won't be charged for them later."

I didn't have to look. I could feel the heat of King's stare on the side of my face. Sartori folded his arms across his chest and eyeballed me.

"Let me get this straight. I don't have to admit to anything that might have happened last night, but if I tell you about others that I maybe did before, you won't charge me for them?"

"Correct. That's the deal. It's a one-time offer that expires the moment we leave this room. You help us clear previous break-ins and you get a pass on them."

Sartori agreed. I told King to fetch the clipboard with the list of break-ins for the last two months. He gawked at me sideways, but did as I asked and returned a few minutes later with the summary sheets. Together, we went through the bar break-ins in the downtown area, and he admitted to seven of them.

At the mention of one particular business, Sartori accused the owner of lying, saying the amount of booze reported stolen was double what he actually took. It was good to know, and not the first time the victim of a break-in fudged the list of stolen items for the insurance money.

Back in the office, after he returned Sartori to the cellblock, King asked me to explain what went down in the interview room. He was impressed at how I got the man to open up and talk but didn't understand the free pass on his other crimes.

"Think about it, Mike. He never admitted to the current crime, but he confirmed the types of businesses he hits, how he gets in, and what he takes. We have a good case on the one he's under arrest for...whether or not he confessed to it. Who knows if we could ever solve those other cases? Now we have. We clear them to him, with no charges except for todays, and improve our stats at the same time. It's a win-win all the way around."

King stood there and thought about it for a moment, and smiled. "I guess that's why you get the big bucks, eh Storm?"

Four

Funny Money

Willy's place wasn't on my way home. I headed across town and stopped in for a beer to see what was up. He was the younger of my two brothers. I also had three sisters. We chatted for a bit and he bitched about the impending lay-off at the factory where he worked. Willy said it shouldn't be a problem because he'd found a new source of income. The remark piqued my interest and I asked what he meant.

My little brother lifted an ashtray on the coffee table and handed me the hundred-dollar bill concealed under it. I took the note and jokingly asked if his wife had taken to working the street. It was a family joke only we understood.

"What do you think?" He asked.

After a quick examination of the currency, I reached out to hand it to him.

"About what?"

"Do you think it's real?"

Pulling it back, I took a closer look, checking the bill for the security features. Canadian paper money is colored and the one-hundred-dollar bill is brown. I ran the note through my fingers and held it up to the light. I wasn't confident in my expertise, but it felt and looked authentic.

"You think it's fake?" I asked. "Did someone pass it off and you're worried about holding the hot potato? I gotta say...it looks good to me."

"You sure?"

"I dunno, Willy, I'm no expert. Thought you would have passed it off to someone else by now...you getting a conscious?"

"Lisa has a stack of them in her dresser drawer."

She was his stepdaughter through marriage.

"What...where would she get a stack of hundreds...did she rob a bank?"

"We don't know...I'd show you the rest but she'll be home any minute...could be her new 'loser' boyfriend. He doesn't work, but always seems to have money...and now these. I slipped this one out of the wad. She probably won't miss it. Her mother came across the stash while putting laundry away. Can you take it to work and check it out? We'd like to know what the hell she's into."

I had another look at the C-note. I wouldn't have questioned the bill if it was passed to me. The front door opened and Willy cleared his throat. I stuffed the hundred in my pocket. Lisa said a quick 'hello uncle' on her way through the room, and headed upstairs. We made small talk for a few more minutes while I finished my beer. I told my brother dinner was waiting for me at home, and I'd look into it for him when I got back to work.

It was about a forty-minute drive from the cop shop to my house in Colchester, a small village on the north shore of Lake Erie. Stopping at my brother's place added another ten minutes to the trip. I didn't mind the drive. It gave me time to digest my day and consider plans for my Sunday off. It was my short weekend. I worked Saturday and went back in on Monday. Driving through the town of McGregor, I checked the usual sites—the church where I was baptized, the house by the creek where we lived until I was three, and the house where my grandparents lived.

When I hit the open road, my cell phone rang. It was my informant, Joey. He wanted to meet up, saying he had something to show me. I told him I was out of town for the day, which was almost true, and I'd hook up with him on Monday when I got back to work. I was bushed, and didn't feel like driving back into the city. Sometimes CIs needed a reality check. They called at all hours, thinking I worked around the clock, seven days a week.

The smell hit me as soon as I opened the front door. I left a cottage roll in the crock-pot. My wife, Sandra, had gone to visit her best friend in London. She always made sure I had something in the fridge to eat when she went away, but cooking for myself wasn't a big deal. Being the eldest sibling, I made my share of Kraft Dinner and grilled cheese sandwiches when mom was at work.

I let the dog out for a pee and fixed myself a plate. After filling the mutt's bowl, I hit the outside deck, just off the dining room. Brandy checked the yard's perimeter, but made a break for me when she saw her dinner. I took my favorite seat overlooking the pond. It was just after six and the sun had already disappeared behind my house. Old man winter was packing his bags, and moving south.

The koi and goldfish gathered in the shallows near me. They were always hungry. I grabbed a handful of pellets from a can under the table, and tossed them into the water. The feeding frenzy didn't last long. Content for the time being, the fish wandered off to digest their food. A leopard frog nosed up to a pellet sitting on a lily pad, but didn't find it appetizing.

The pond was something I put in during our first year at the Colchester house. Using knowledge gleaned from a landscape design course I took at St. Clair College; I tore up the whole back yard and put in a stream and two-tiered pond with waterfalls. It took me the better part of a two-week furlough and had me trucking in loads of fieldstone from nearby farms. I planted an assortment of perennials and extended the deck with a boardwalk running along the water's edge.

After my last bite, the dinner plate went to Brandy for pre-washing. I filled my lungs with country air and watched an oriole, standing on a rock, drink from the lower pond. Reaching down I petted the dog. She had her eye on something moving in the grass. It was Fat Frank, our resident bullfrog. He liked to visit the neighbor's pond across the street during the day, but returned home for the night. Life was good in my back yard.

Five

Far & Away

Chen Shen vomited for two days. At least that's how long she thought it had been. It was hard to tell. Very little light came in through the two vents in the ceiling. There were nineteen other girls with her, most were older, but a few younger. One said she felt seasick and thought they might be on a boat.

The ceiling, floor, and walls of the room were made of steel and became hot when it was light and cold when it was dark. There was no furniture, only a large plastic water jug, and two pails used as toilets. Both were almost full, causing some of the girls to pee in the corner, or simply relieve themselves in their clothes. The stench made Chen's eyes water.

At least another two days went by without food. Some of the girls had fought over what was left of the water the day before. Chen thought about her last meal, just before she was taken from her home. She wished she'd eaten her vegetables and finished the noodles. Her stomach had stopped growling long ago. It felt hollow now, as if everything had pulled inside to keep her alive.

The girls who fought over the water, congregated in their own corner, eyeing the others and whispering among themselves. It was survival of the fittest. Chen imagined the worst. They might kill someone for their flesh. She scanned the other faces in the room. Some girls stared into empty space, and others slept forever. She wondered if they were still alive.

Her best guess; this was the fifth day. The steal room suddenly lurched sideways, spilling the pails of excrement all over the floor and the two closest girls. One of them dry-heaved, but the other never moved. Chen surmised she was either unconscious or dead. She heard voices outside, and the sound of a metal latch at the opposite end.

Half of the wall opened allowing in bright light, blinding her. Chen shielded her eyes. She heard the voices of men, yelling at them to get up and come out. Before she could climb to her feet, a strong hand grabbed her arm and pulled her up. Her legs wobbled as if made of rubber, and she struggled to keep her balance. A man pulled her into the light. Looking down to put one foot in front of the other, she saw another man kick two of the girls who weren't moving.

Stepping outside the door, Chen blinked hard trying to focus on where they were. She felt the warmth of the sun on her face. The air was hot and humid but smelled better than inside. The stench lingered and she thought it was probably her own clothes and body odor. They paraded the girls down a row of huge steel containers.

With his giant paw clamped on her arm, the man took most of her weight. Her feet barely touched the ground as they moved forward. Chen heard a bird, possibly a seagull. She turned and caught a glimpse of water, but the man pulled a hood over her head. She guessed they were on a boat, and had been inside one of those big metal boxes. She had no idea where they were.

She heard the sounds of machinery and other men. She was lifted and tossed into another metal box. Her hood slipped and she counted five other girls. The doors slammed shut. Chen saw enough to know she was inside a truck. What she didn't know, was where she was or where she was going.

Six

Criminal Injustice System

I was scheduled to work the night shift on Monday, but had a 10am court appearance. It was a drug trial for a dealer we'd busted almost two years before. It wasn't unusual for cases to take that long getting to court. Especially for jury trials held in Superior Court. Normally, criminal defense lawyers delayed the inevitable, keeping their clients on the street as long as possible.

Checking in at the office first, I asked my boss if I could start my shift whenever court recessed for the day. He agreed, being flexible that way. It was better for me since I was already in the city and didn't have to make another trip home and back.

The Drug Squad was next door to our office and I went there to visit my buddy, Blackjack. He was the officer in charge of our court case. Blackjack was the same rank as me, but classified as sergeant because of his supervisory role in the Drug Squad. We had both worked there as constables, and became friends. He was fiddling with the knot in his tie when I walked into his office.

"Heard anything about the case...what we can expect?" I asked.

"Just from my CI...she's scared shitless her dealer will find out she gave him up. The asshole called her and said his lawyer was going to find out who ratted him out. You and I know I'd never give up her name, but she said his lawyer and the judge stay at the same place in Florida."

"Fuck me. That's not good."

The trial was actually a continuance requested by the sitting judge. Defense counsel asked Blackjack who his informant was when he was on the witness stand. When he refused to answer the question, opposing counsels got into a heated discussion over whether or not he had to reveal his source. It was a tight spot to be in, but historically police sources were protected and their identities do not have to be revealed.

It was nothing new for my buddy, or I. We'd seen lawyers do it. It didn't matter what the accused did, it was all about finding out who ratted on them. We knew some lawyers had their clients pay for the privilege of getting the information, even though the lawyer had no way to physically obtain it. CI names were left out of the paperwork for exactly that reason.

I felt sorry for the informant. She was close to the dealer she gave up, and there he was telling her his lawyer knew the Judge and was going to get him the rat's name. Before the trial started, Blackjack was called into the judge's chambers, without the criminal lawyer or Crown Attorney present.

The so-called 'Honorable Judge' asked the sergeant directly who his informant was, saying he had to know so he could make his own decision on the reliability of the information. He threatened Blackjack with contempt of court if he didn't provide the name. It was complete bullshit, and he should never have put a police officer in that position. My buddy held his ground and refused to reveal the name of his source.

The jury remained in the dark during all of the pre-trial discussions. At the end of the trial, the judge called us liars, and instructed the jury to disregard our testimony. In other words, he blatantly told them to acquit. It was a good case. We had solid information and I found the drugs after watching the dealer drop them in the snow.

Juries are unpredictable and our judge took no chances. They deliberated and returned to court within the hour. We held our breath. I would never have believed what happened next if I wasn't there to witness it myself. The jury returned with a verdict of not guilty, but a female juror in the front row noticeably shook her head in disagreement, as the foreman read their decision.

The Crown Attorney caught the woman's gesture and asked the judge to poll the jurors to see if they all agreed with the verdict. The law calls for a unanimous decision. It was his honor's duty to ask each juror individually, but he addressed the group as a whole. Most heads nodded in response but the woman juror, who had shaken her head, fainted.

The Judge ordered the courtroom cleared immediately and a few of us went to the woman's aid. She came to within a minute and we sat her up. The first words out of her mouth were, 'some of us knew he was guilty but the others wouldn't let us vote that way—we had no say'. After twenty-four years on the job, I thought I'd seen and heard it all. I was wrong.

Blackjack and I were upset and expressed our concerns to the boss. He only shrugged and said we should leave it to the Crown Attorney. The Federal Prosecutor who tried the case said he never experienced such an injustice, and would be seeking an appeal. It never happened, and he left the law firm shortly thereafter.

The good news was the informant's identity was never revealed. The bad news was the drug dealer laughed at us and walked away. Almost...he had to pay his lawyer $30,000 for that freedom, and we kept his dope.

Seven

Back to Work

I couldn't stop shaking my head. After spending a full and exhausting day in court, I went back to work to hunt down and capture more bad guys, who could game the system...and people wonder why cops drink. After dumping the suit in my locker, I hit our gym for a workout and chance to clear my head. It didn't help.

The day shift was gone by the time I got into the office. It was just as well; I couldn't stop replaying the day's events, and didn't feel like repeating the story again. Instead, I checked my phone messages, email, and cell phone. Someone left a message while I was in the gym.

Willy had called, wanting to know if I checked into the hundred-dollar bill yet. I glanced at the wall clock, but the fraud detectives were gone for the day. I took the note out of my wallet and had another look at it.

They had taught us the basics at Police College, like how to use your thumbnail to feel the raised ink. We also learned to scratch off the planchettes; the little green dots that appear randomly on paper money. There was also micro printing that was difficult to duplicate. The weight and texture of the paper felt right but I didn't see any green dots.

It was a problem on larger bills. They could have been scraped off by someone else checking the bill's authenticity. Deciding to leave it with the experts, I left a phone message with one of the fraud detectives, put the bill in an envelope, and slipped it into their mail slot.

My crew wasn't due in until six. I called my CI, Joey, to see if he still wanted to meet up. He was a cocaine dealer who I busted when I was in the Drug Squad. After working off his charges by giving up other drug traffickers, Joey stayed in touch hoping my co-workers wouldn't come after him again. He learned valuable lessons from his arrest...getting smarter so he could continue to sell drugs. After I transferred to Street Crimes, his illegal activities were someone else's problem.

We met in a bowling alley parking lot. After some small talk, Joey peeled off two one-hundred-dollar bills from his wad of cash and handed them to me. When I asked what they were for, he said they were fake. Once again, the bills could have fooled me.

"The paper and texture are off." He said, "And the foil security patch isn't right."

He took another note from his roll and gave it to me for comparison. I rubbed it between my fingers and examined it closely. The two bills he gave me were newer, and the serial numbers were different. I wasn't sure of their authenticity but Joey swore they were counterfeit.

"I handle cash all day and these bills are bogus...the different thickness of paper jammed my money counter."

"You have a fucking machine to count your money?"

Joey shrugged.

"Where'd you get the C notes?"

"Guy at the strip club...slipped them in with the real ones when he paid me."

He never told me who his drug clients were, but I asked anyway.

"What guy at which club?"

Joey smiled and paused a second.

"One of the guys who owns T & A...he runs a tight ship and would rather sell dope to the girls himself than have outside dealers come in and bring heat to the club. Keep the bills and have someone check them out...it's not like I can call the cops and say the guy ripped me off."

I slipped the notes into my shirt pocket and told him I'd look into it. He stuffed his roll of cash back into his pocket. When I asked what he was doing with all the money he was making, Joey said he paid cash for everything—even his leased car, but he was looking at investing in a legit business to launder his drug money.

"I even paid income tax this year to keep the government off my back...they don't seem to care how you make a living, just as long as they get their piece of the pie."

Wondering for a second if I chose the wrong profession, I told Joey I had to go, since I had a real job. He wished me luck with that.

Eight

Late-Night Drive Through

Having started my shift ahead of time, I thought I'd go home early. It had been a quiet night. I caught up the paperwork, while two of my crew drove the street. It was just after midnight, and I was locking up my desk, when a dispatcher called me. King and Gelinas stopped a suspicious vehicle coming out of a South Windsor subdivision. King had a keen eye for such things and thought he recognized a passenger in the car.

Both cops had ten years on the job, with no investigative experience before their transfer to Street Crimes. They needed little supervision, and although they had completely different personalities, the two worked well together. King was short, stocky, and generally kept to himself. Gelinas, a bit softer and curvier, was the mother of two when she wasn't at work.

The three male suspects cruised slowly through an upscale neighborhood hours after dark. Upon checking the license plate, Gelinas confirmed the vehicle belonged to a criminal with a record for B & E. He was a repeat offender and on our radar since his release from prison. I asked the dispatcher to have one of my crew call me, so I knew whether to stay or go home.

King called five minutes later. He arrested Samir Sarkis for breaching his curfew and being in possession of B & E tools. He thought the latter charge might be a stretch and a difficult one to prove, but it was reason enough to get a convicted criminal, who was up to no good, off the street. Considering his past record and the circumstances involved, I agreed and we went ahead with the charges.

The other two young men in the car were also arrested and the vehicle was impounded. Our records indicated one of the other men had a record for property crimes, but the youngest passenger had no previous criminal convictions. He was Sarkis' cousin. I unlocked my desk and started to prepare the arrest file for arraignment court in the morning.

Samir was well known to the police, and I'd arrested him once before for possession of stolen property. One of my informants told me Sarkis had a bunch of high-end stolen jewelry he was trying to sell to a jewelry store. Lucky for me Samir had an arrest warrant at the time, giving me probable cause to stop his car and not burn my informant.

I put together a package for the Mobile Surveillance Unit and they tried to follow Sarkis, but his counter-surveillance techniques made it impossible for them to do their job without being compromised. He drove at high speeds, sometimes with his lights off in the dark, and blew through traffic signals to spot or lose any potential police tails.

When King and Gelinas came into the office, I told them to conduct the interviews while I put together their court package. It was doubtful Sarkis would admit to anything, but with criminal charges held over their heads, there was always the possibility one of the other two might have something to say. When all was said and done, they gave us nothing.

It was almost 2am, when my cell phone rang. The call display said 'unknown caller' but that was normal. Another of my informants, Ham, asked if I was working. I said of course or I wouldn't have answered his call at that time of the morning. Ham's proper name was Mohamed something-something Mohamed, in Arabic. I shortened it. He was the same CI who gave me the tip on the variety store and massage parlor.

Before I mentioned anything about it, Ham said he knew we busted Samir and his cousin. He didn't know the other guy, and said he was a friend of the cousins. When I asked how he knew what was going on, Ham said some of the jewelry from their take was supposed to come his way. Apparently, the cops spooked them and they didn't pull their job.

He went on to tell me how Sarkis scoped out potential targets during the day, checking for extra satellite dishes on upscale houses, apparently meaning the occupants were Middle Eastern people who liked to keep high-end jewelry and cash in their homes. If the occupants appeared to be away, the bandits returned at night and broke in. Some of the information was new to me, especially the part about the satellite dishes. Normally, the majority of residential break-ins occurred during the day, while homeowners were at work.

Ham told me we needed to do a better job following Sarkis and his crew. They knew all of our unmarked cars from driving around the police station and copying down license plates. Certain vehicles were kept underground and off-site but I didn't tell him that. It was obvious Samir was smarter than most criminals. It was either good police work or just dumb luck, King and Gelinas found him before his next score.

I told my CI I'd talk with him later. I had to finish the paperwork and go home to bed. He said he'd check in with me the next day, and let me know if he heard anything more from Samir or his guys.

Nine

Next Stop

Chen didn't say a word inside the truck. A man lifted her hood and dumped bottled water down her throat. She gagged and spit up more than she was able to swallow. He offered no food. She couldn't remember how long it had been since she had eaten. For something to do, Chen imagined her favorite meals, cooked by her mother at home. She missed her family.

It seemed like they drove forever. When the vehicle finally stopped, the doors opened and she heard voices. More rough hands pawed at her tiny arms, pulling her out of the truck. Her feet landed on gravel. She could see out of the bottom of her hood. Chen heard one girl scream, and what sounded like someone landing a blow to the girl's head. A sharp voice rang out; a woman speaking in a different dialect. It sounded like she was scolding the man who hit the girl.

They went inside a building and down a set of stairs. Chen felt cool damp air. The room was so poorly lit she could barely see her feet. Someone pushed her up against a hard wall and yanked off the hood. Her eyes focused on an attractive Asian woman she'd never seen before. The other girls flanked Chen, two on each side. She took in the room. It was a place she'd never forget.

The thin woman, her arms folded across her chest, stood facing the girls. The man who removed their hoods stood at her side. The woman demanded the girls remove their clothes. Her words were difficult for Chen to understand, but she got the message. The younger girl to her right froze and broke down crying. The man stepped forward and ripped off her clothes with one swipe.

Once they were all naked, he kicked their soiled clothes into a corner. The woman pushed open a door behind her and told the girls to go inside. Chen and three others complied but the last girl was still in shock, and they dragged her in by her hair. It was a smaller room with the same bare cement walls. The single light bulb, hanging from the ceiling, barely lit the space. The woman hit a switch on the wall and a steel showerhead came to life. She gave the tallest girl a bar of soap and ordered them all to wash themselves.

The door closed, leaving the girls naked and alone. Chen could barely stand her own body odor. She thought it had been her clothes. She took the soap and stepped into the shower. The water was cold but it made her feel alive again. She lathered herself from head to toe, and handed off the soap. The other girls followed her lead. Exiting the shower, Chen grabbed the only towel. It hung on the wall hook near another door. She dried herself the best she could before a bigger girl grabbed the towel. Wet, cold, hungry, and lost, Chen shivered and fought to hold her tears. Something told her there would be time for crying later.

The door beside the towel hook opened, and the same woman called Chen into the adjoining room. The new space was brighter and felt a bit warmer, but surrounded by the same gray walls. There was a rectangular steel table in the middle of the space, and an older grey-haired Asian man standing behind it. He wore a white coat, like her doctor, and he had one of those things around his neck he used to listen to her chest. She cowered near the door, trying to cover the private area between her legs.

The doctor pointed to the table. He spoke in the same dialect as the woman. Chen knew what he meant, but not what was about to happen. The woman told her to lay face up on the table and be still. She complied but kept her hands over the area below her belly button. The table was ice-cold. The bright light seemed to give off some heat. She pretended it was the sun and imagined she was at the beach.

The man examined her closely, like her mother's doctor had done once before. He checked her eyes, ears, and mouth. The listening device was cold, but his hands felt warm and smooth. They worked their way down her body, from her armpits and across her tummy. Chen tensed when he grabbed her knees and tried to spread her legs apart.

He was too strong to resist and she submitted. The doctor's fingers probed places no one else had ever touched. He didn't say a word but glanced at the woman and nodded. She was expressionless, but appeared satisfied and ordered Chen off the table and through the door behind her.

It led to another gloomy room with more cold and hard walls. There were six small mattresses laid out on the floor, with a set of fresh clothes and a folded blanket placed in the middle of each one. Chen chose the bed furthest from the door and grabbed the clothes. There was nothing else in the room except a familiar-looking bucket in the opposite corner.

A wooden stairway ran up one wall. After all the girls were in the room and dressed, a young man came down the stairs with a box of sandwiches and bottles of water. The girls almost knocked him over, trying to get at the food.

Ten

Phone Tag

I was on the night shift and the Fraud Unit worked steady days. We took turns leaving each other phone messages. They confirmed the hundred-dollar bills were counterfeit and wanted to know what they should do with them; if there was a case number or complainant. Their office also received a few of the bogus notes, which they described as high quality, from a downtown bank. They had no idea where the fake bills were coming from and asked if I could get any more information from my sources.

The night shift was my favorite to work. It was quieter in the building, with less brass around. I enjoyed sleeping in and having the whole day to run errands, work in the garden, and get things done. At work, there was more time to catch up on paperwork, and it was easier to meet up with informants who didn't get their ass out of bed until after noon.

I called my little brother but his wife said he was working afternoons too. She asked if there was a message. I said it was about Lisa and the hundred-dollar bill. Sharlene told me she hadn't seen her daughter in days. She took off with her boyfriend. The wad of cash in her drawer was gone too. My sister-in-law said I should sit Lisa down and read her the riot act. I wasn't a father but knew how that would go; trying to tell a teenager what to do.

My next call was to Joey. He answered on the first ring. With all the drug dealers I had met on the job, Joey was the most punctual one. He was a true entrepreneur who didn't use his own product. He chose to stuff his pockets with cash instead. He asked if I looked into the C-notes and I told him there were others floating around the city.

"Why don't you meet me at the strip bar, and see what's going on for yourself?"

"Joey, as much as I enjoy eyeballing naked women, I'm not sure it's a good idea for us to be seen together."

"I know...we don't have to sit together. I'll just nod or casually point out the owner...the one who dumped the bogus bills on me. His first name is Rick. You should look him up."

I thought about his idea and what other work we had on our agenda for the night. King was single and made a good wing man. Kristen Gelinas wasn't the peeler-bar kind of woman. Joey went on with his sales pitch but I cut him off, saying I'd get back to him later if I could make it work. Technically, checking a licensed liquor establishment fell under the Morality Unit's umbrella, and they were off for the night. I could probably sell it to my boss, but only after the fact.

It was too early to hit the strip bar. I brought up my caseload on the computer. I had twelve open files on the go. The number was a bit high for a supervisor. All of my cases were B & E related. Four of them were tied together by a reverse hit on AFIS—the Canadian criminal database for fingerprints. A reverse hit meant a fresh set of prints input into the system matched others previously collected at a crime scene.

Computers solving crime was a new and invaluable concept. It was used to solve old cases where the suspect had no prints on file when the offence was committed. In my case, the AFIS hit came up two years after the original break-ins. I always loved the look on a dirtbag's face when they heard they were under arrest for something they thought they got away with years ago; the long arm of the law and all that.

I spent time typing up supplementary reports and was able to close two of my files. Taking advantage of a lull in the action, I went down to the basement for a workout. We had a great gym designed and stocked by my best friend, Jesse. Our police association split the cost with the police service and Jesse went on a shopping spree, purchasing top-notch weight training and cardio equipment.

When I returned to the office after my workout, King and Gelinas had their faces buried in paperwork. After dropping my gym bag beside my desk, I headed for the fridge to grab my lunch. Kristen stopped me on the way by.

"Do you think I can get the last couple hours off tonight? I have a continuation in court in the morning."

Reactively, I glanced to the clock. "Sure, I don't see why not." A smile cracked my face.

"What?" Gelinas asked, looking puzzled.

"Nothing, I was just thinking of something else."

King caught the conversation and the expression on my face. I winked at him and continued on to my desk. I saw them eyeballing each other, both intrigued. He shrugged and they returned to their work. Deciding I wasn't in the mood to write more reports, I ate my lunch and checked my email for jokes and non-work-related stuff.

Gelinas packed up her desk and brought me the time off book. We used it to log overtime hours collected in-office, and appease the bean counters who constantly bitched about the overtime budget. I opened the book to her page and seeing her accumulated hours were in the black, left the total unchanged. Kristen smiled and said thank you. It was my way of saying thanks for her hard work and the little extras.

When the office door closed behind her, I told King to finish what he was doing as I had a follow-up to take care of. Investigators teamed up most of the time when they went on the road. King followed my lead without question. He clipped his holster onto his belt and grabbed a portable radio from the cabinet. I locked the office door behind us and off we went.

Michael King wasn't a big talker. In the car, he listened to the police radio and looked out his window. This kind of alone time with my subordinates allowed me to feel them out and test their satisfaction level with the job. The man had willingly accepted and excelled at every challenge I threw at him.

He'd done a bang-up job with the Rub n' Tug project. Besides his marital status, the only other things I knew about King was he liked to hunt and he lived in the county with his hunting dog. I asked if he had plans to go up north for the upcoming killing season and he nodded. His expression barely changed when I pulled into the parking lot at the T & A Gentlemen's club.

"Thought you had a follow-up?"

I raised my eyebrows in acknowledgement.

"This is it. Call it a bar check for the morality guys...one of my CIs says the owner passed him some bogus C-notes."

King reached for his door handle.

"Leave the gun and radio, we're going incognito."

Eleven

The Windsor Ballet

In jeans and collared shirts, King and I looked pretty well the same as all the other horndogs in T & A. Grabbing a seat at a table near the back wall separated us from those in pervert row, their chairs right in front of the stage. Strip bars weren't my thing but I'd been in many of them over the years. Earlier in my career, when I worked off duty in bars, I saw Windsor's first male strippers.

One woman offered me money if I shed my uniform on stage. I told her she couldn't afford me. It amazed me how women were actually more promiscuous and rambunctious then men. One woman s removed from the stage when she tried to join the show. Others let dancers stir their drinks with their dicks. The woman who wanted me to dance hung around until the end of the night and invited herself home with me. I was single at the time and obliged.

A mix of female dancers worked the stage and prowled the room at T & A. King and I waved off two tattooed and weathered vultures before we were able to flag down a waitress. He gave me a questionable look when I ordered a drink, but I told him it was okay—we had to blend in to keep our cover. He attempted to pay for his drink but I got both and said they were on the company. Mike smiled and asked when there would be an opening in Morality.

On the outside, strip bars resembled lots of other buildings throughout the city, but on the inside, they were all dark and dingy. It wasn't done to set the mood; it often hid just how ugly some of the women truly were. They all looked toned and tanned in the right light. The brass pole and elevated stage at the T & A resembled every other club in the country.

I scanned the room and spotted my CI, Joey. He had mostly naked women on each side of him. Like sharks who could smell blood a mile away, seasoned strippers clung to men with money like wet t-shirts. One of the women he was with looked familiar to me. Joey saw me and lifted his head to acknowledge my presence. The peeler noticed the gesture, and squinted to get a better image of me. Never one to forget a face, I couldn't remember where I met her. She was too young to have danced at the place where I worked off duty years earlier. It would come to me.

King checked out the woman on stage, who wore nothing but a gold scarf that reminded me of something we wrapped around the Christmas tree as kids. Once called Sin City of the North, Windsor is one of the few places where dancers could shed all but one item of clothing. It didn't leave much to the imagination.

A well-dressed man about my age brushed my elbow on his way to the bar. He'd just come from the office. I wondered if he was Rick, the owner Joey told me about. A quick glance his way and a nod from him, said I had the right guy. I'd never seen him before. The name Rick was not on the liquor license, only a numbered company. The Liquor Inspector would be able to tell me more.

The familiar-looking dancer left Joey's table and casually made her way to ours. She kept her eyes on me but asked Mike if he wanted a lap dance. Caught off guard, he blushed and politely declined the offer. I told him he could have a dance if he wanted to keep his cover and we could justify the expense to the boss if he could get her to solicit him for sex in the VIP room. King stared back at me, wondering if I was serious.

It wasn't something that normally took place in strip clubs, but it did happen. I played the role once for the Morality Squad, posing as a client at a massage parlor. The goal was to be solicited by the masseuse without actually letting them complete the sex act. That's unless you were Shorty, my partner. He said that nobody told him he was supposed to stop the woman from giving him a happy ending. They never charged the woman for fear he'd have to tell all in open court.

It came to me. I remembered her name was Roxanne and I busted her for possession when we raided a shooting gallery—a house where needle users went to score and get high. Having a search warrant for the residence meant we could arrest and search everyone who was present. Roxanne was in possession of Dilaudid, a heroin substitute. She only had a few pills and traded information to avoid being charged. The woman had a good job and didn't want a criminal record.

I watched her expression change from puzzlement to acknowledgement as she left our table. She'd remembered too, and broke eye contact when she realized who I was. Her hair was different, shorter and darker, and she gained some weight in the right places. It was the first time I saw her without clothes, and she was pretty hot for her age, if I remembered it correctly.

It would have been easy enough to strike up a conversation with Roxanne, to see how life was and all that, but I left it alone. It was impossible to get a read on her in that short visit, and there was no reason for her to talk to me anymore. She owed me nothing.

Rick took a wad of cash from the register and walked by us on the way to the office. I couldn't help but wonder how many fake hundreds were making their way around the place. When I turned my head back to Mike, Roxanne was sitting between us with a fresh drink in front of her.

"Hey Storm, how's it hanging?"

Twelve

Surprises

The next morning was routine. I slept in, read the paper at the dining room table, and gazed out the patio doors at the pond. I fed the dog, cat, birds, fish, and myself. The neighbor and her daughter waved from the driveway on their way out. I was washing my breakfast dishes when the phone rang. Drying my hands on a dishtowel, I grabbed the extension and sat back down at the table. A squirrel discovered the fresh birdseed I just put out...little bastard.

Willy was on the phone. He said Lisa was busted in Toronto for passing counterfeit money and spent the night in jail. His stepdaughter knew better than to call home and an aunt who lived up there, bailed her out. He said she hadn't returned home yet, and asked if there was anything I could do.

"Like what?" I asked. "That's way out of my jurisdiction."

"Can you talk to her when she gets home...maybe she'll tell you something and you can put in a good word with the cops up there. She will never get a decent job with a criminal record."

I thought about whether it was even possible to make a long-distance deal like that with another police force.

"We'll see little brother. I don't have any connections in T.O. but I'll run it buy the guys in the Fraud Squad. All the deals I've made with informants in the past have been local. Give me a shout when she comes home, and I'll take it from there."

"Okay, thanks. You still on afternoons...what are you up to?"

"Not much...there's an old woman and a toddler standing beside the pond. Gotta go...our mother is on my deck."

"Tell her I said hello."

"Tell her yourself, it's your turn to take her for groceries. She was in the store for hours last time I took her. I went to the gym, ran some errands, and she still wasn't done when I went to pick her up."

"You're the oldest, it's your responsibility. What were you thinking when you moved so close to her?"

Willy hung up and I went outside to see what mom was up to. She lived down the street, a few houses from the lake. We were both into gardening. She checked to see what was in bloom while the rug-rat talked to the fish. He made a move at the water's edge and she grabbed him by the arm. He was one of the kids she babysat. My mother's house was the neighborhood daycare center.

She looked frailer than how I remembered her growing up. Larger than life itself most of the time, my mother accepted every challenge that came her way with little complaint. She wasn't happy about having cancer. In remission now, the first round of chemo and radiation took a lot out of her. She was a year shy of her first government pension check and the European dream trip she was planning.

We chatted some and I filled her in about the problems with Lisa. My mother said she wouldn't be like that if the girl came to her boot camp. Her house was a penal colony of sorts, where my other brother sent his boys when they got out of control. Mom put them to work from sunrise to sundown, driving them like slaves and getting them to do her chores. Even the neighborhood parents who left their kids with her, commented on how disciplined they were after leaving my mother's house.

That was Mom. A strong-willed woman who had been a schoolteacher before six kids took over her life. My father leaving and her taking on two jobs to make ends meet, made her even tougher. When I joked about growing bigger and carrying a gun, she said it wouldn't matter if she clocked me from behind with a two-by-four. Some would call that child abuse but we all turned out fine.

The little nipper got whiney and mom said they were heading back home. Before leaving the yard, she asked when we were going for groceries next. I said I just talked to Willy on the phone and he said he'd love to take her and to give him a call. She walked down the neighbor's driveway mumbling something about having at least one good son. I knew she still loved me. I sat for a second to take in autumn's bounty. It was my garden's last hurrah before winter.

The previous night's conversation with Roxanne played in my mind. We had chatted and caught up while King eavesdropped and watched the stage show. He seemed to enjoy the free drinks and entertainment. My former CI confirmed Rick owned the bar and had a silent partner. She knew he dealt coke to some of the girls, but nothing about any funny money.

The phone rang and I went into the house to answer it. A woman asked for me by name and said I didn't know her. She was calling for a friend, whose husband had spent the night out of town, with my wife. Not knowing what to say, I instinctively glanced at the door to the garage. Sandra was at work. My brain jumped into high gear and I asked who was calling and why. The woman repeated the message and said I should ask my wife where she was this past weekend. Then she hung up.

Thirteen

Home Sweet Home

Realizing they were all in the same predicament, the girls began to talk amongst themselves. It started with sharing their first names, and where they lived before being abducted. The oldest-looking one remained silent and quaked at the slightest sound. She cowered whenever the young man delivered their food. Chen thought something bad must have happened to her.

The girls all spoke Chinese, but only one used the same dialect as her. They were all from different places around the country. One said something in English, but Chen didn't respond, being unsure of exactly how much about herself she should share with strangers. She feared the future, not knowing whom to trust.

There were no windows in the room so days and nights ran together. The delivery of their meals and the light switching on and off gave them the only sense of time. If the newspapers beside their commode were recent, she missed her birthday. Chen had just turned thirteen. There was no singing or cake, only bread and water and occasionally dry meat sandwiches.

The group tried to engage the quiet girl, but she was traumatized and beyond any help they could offer. It was a shame. She was the tallest and easily the prettiest of the group. One of the Mandarin girls called her Angel. Even though Chen spoke Shanghainese, she was able to communicate with the others.

She attempted to keep track of what she thought to be the number of days and weeks in captivity by scratching stick lines on the cement wall. If Chen was right, it was on the 10th day the food deliveryman took Angel upstairs. They all guessed at where she was and what might happen to her, but nobody had any idea.

Angel didn't return until the next morning. Black and blue from wearing makeup, and crying, streaked her face. She wore a pretty yellow dress, torn on one shoulder, and soiled near the bottom. Chen thought it looked like dried blood. Angel used the railing to steady herself on the stairs and had difficulty walking to her bed. She laid down with her back to the other girls, and cried herself to sleep.

They whispered to each other trying to imagine what happened. One of them said she was probably raped. At her age, Chen wasn't sure exactly what that meant, but it didn't sound good. She grew tense and wasn't sure if it was fear or horror she was feeling. She heard wood creak and the girls went silent as all eyes averted to the stairway.

Fourteen

Fog

I wasn't able to form a complete thought in my head after the strange phone call. The nineteen years, of what I thought was a good marriage, flashed through my brain. Our relationship wasn't perfect, but Sandra never expressed any concerns about being happy. I'd always been faithful and she was the last person on earth who I'd pick to have an affair.

I couldn't help but think about some of my friends and co-workers whose marriages failed for a variety of reasons. In many cases, it was because of infidelity. I thought the mysterious caller might be someone I pissed off on the job, and this was a way of getting even. Not my wife, it simply couldn't be.

The next few hours were a blur and it was while I was getting ready for work that my cop instinct kicked in. Negative thoughts flowed through my head, and I began to question everything. Her suitcase...she had flown to Toronto, or so she had told me. I checked the luggage tag still attached to the suitcase handle. It read New York.

Something started to burn, deep inside my stomach. I drove to work but didn't remember the trip there. My partner and our whole crew were working—it was an overlap day. Office chatter drifted through the fog and into my ears. I heard what was being said, but couldn't focus on the words.

Someone called my name and snapped me out of my stupor. Shorty's crew had a search warrant ready to go and he wanted to brief everyone on the case. I listened. The target was a known fence who was supposed to be sitting on a garage full of stolen property, power tools, and construction supplies. His crew would handle the warrant and arrest. King, Gelinas, and I were part of the search team. We drove there together.

The tip was accurate and the fence arrested with a garage full of hot goods, many items stolen from local construction sites. I wandered around looking at nothing in particular. King started to tell me something about a certain break-in he remembered, but stopped short and asked if I was okay.

"No, sorry, I'm not. Tell Shorty I'm going home sick. You and Gelinas can get a ride back with them."

King looked as though I'd just asked him for the formula for rocket fuel. I turned and headed for the car.

Back at HQ, I stopped to see the Staff Sergeant in charge, and asked him for the master key because I'd locked myself out of the office and the others were at a crime scene. I used the key to enter my wife's office. I was on autopilot, my investigative skills kept me focused on uncovering the truth. Bits and pieces of information came together after I found notations on her calendar and several emails between my wife and another man I knew. They were having an affair.

Fifteen

Coping

Work proved to be a distraction from my marital situation. Down time led to negative thoughts, which only begot more negative thoughts. It was a runaway train with me picturing, imagining, and suspecting the worst. Although easier said, than done, trying not to think about it was the best solution.

An emotional week of confrontation, accusation, and deliberation, stressed me to the point of losing weight. I don't recommend it as a diet solution. Finding myself alone in the office with King and Gelinas, I apologized for being out of sorts and not myself, and admitted to having some problems at home. Surprisingly, they hadn't noticed anything unusual in my behavior. Turns out I was a good faker, and able to keep my negative feelings to myself.

There was no shortage of crime in the city, meaning the number of break-ins kept us busy in Street Crimes. I'd slacked off in the past week, dodging phone calls, and not properly following up perspective leads on my investigative files. Call me selfish. I couldn't help thinking my personal life was more important, than introducing dirtbag's to the revolving door of the justice system.

It was uncharacteristic for me. I completely ignored two of Joey's phone calls and even put off Willy's message coaxing me to speak with Lisa. Waking up emotionally drained every day, I felt like I lost my will to deal with people on a personal level. It was strange...no one picked up on that.

The phone call from Roxanne got me back into the game. She wanted to meet and said the club brought in a bunch of Asian dancers. She thought they weren't legal. It wasn't hard to see that she was afraid of the new competition. I decided to bring Gelinas with me, figuring I could list her as a second handler if Roxanne wanted to get on our payroll again.

We met in a Tim Horton's parking lot near the strip club where Roxanne worked. The two women checked each other out as I made the introductions. I could only imagine what they thought of each other and their chosen professions. The exotic dancer wasted no time in producing a one-hundred-dollar bill she had concealed in her bra.

"Check this out, Storm, I think it's one of the fakes you told me about."

I took the suspected funny money and checked it, keeping in mind what the fraud guys told me. It was counterfeit. I passed the note to Kristen.

Roxanne objected. "I need that back. I've got bills to pay."

Gelinas looked to me for direction before giving it up.

"Roxanne," I said. "It's evidence. If you pass it on to someone else, you're committing a crime. Did Rick give it to you?"

"One of my customers, that's how he paid for his lap dances. I don't think he was trying to rip me off...he's a regular I've known for a long time. He probably thought it was real, he's tipped me big like that before."

I thought about it before I answered.

"Okay, I'll tell you what I'll do. We might be able to cover your loss. I'll write it up as a payoff for information on the club. But we'll need more...you gotta get some dirt on the owner."

"That's why I called you...he brought in a bunch of new dancers...Asian girls."

She continued but my phone rang. I told Gelinas to take notes while I stepped out of the car to take the call. Roxanne shrugged and continued.

Ham was on the phone. He wasn't one for small talk and got to the point. He told me Samir Sarkis was out on bail and back at it, doing B & E's. It didn't surprise me. The justice system was a joke to career criminals like Sarkis, who knew how to work it to their advantage. Just keep pleading not guilty to charges, promise to come back to court, abide by imposed conditions that will never be followed, and continue to commit crime.

It was job security for cops like me. Ham said Samir figured he could go about six months, before he'd have to face up to his charges and do some time. He knew exactly how to game the system—plead guilty to one charge and in exchange have the Prosecutor drop the others. It was the way of the world. We called it 'Let's Make a Deal'.

Sarkis offered my CI first dibs on the high-end jewelry he planned to score from the B & E's he had planned. Being close to the thief, Ham provided me with descriptions of three different vehicles that Samir used to commit the break-ins, and where he kept them parked. I considered his tip and said how difficult it was to follow Sarkis when he was on the prowl.

Ham suggested we put a tracker on his car. He would be able to tell us which one Samir would be driving. He answered my next question, how we would know which car to follow. The other question in my mind was how we would be able to attach the tracking device and if we'd have enough advance notice to install it.

My CI continued telling me how to do my job, suggesting we watch the parking lot where Samir's cars were parked, to see which ones he used and how we'd be able to plant our bug. I wondered to myself why Ham wasn't a cop himself, having to admit that he had some very good ideas. No one else at the cop shop had thought about using a tracking device. I said I'd get back to him about Sarkis and the tracker.

When I climbed back into the car Roxanne was on her way out. She said her break was over and she had to get back to work. Gelinas gave me a nod to let me know she had it under control. The dancer turned to me before shutting her door.

"You owe me a hundred bucks', copper."

I offered a flat smile and my advice. "Go shake your booty...you'll make it back in no time."

Roxanne shot me the finger. Gelinas laughed.

"She's quite a character, Norm. I've never had a serious conversation with a stripper before."

"You mean exotic dancer."

"Whatever."

"Did she have anything useful to say...what about the Asian dancers?"

"Complaining mostly...apparently, the owner has brought in some new girls, all Asian, from Montreal. She says he's putting them up in a house, and keeping their immigration papers until they pay back whatever they owe for their trip to Canada."

"I understand her beef. Perverts like seeing fresh meat...something strange and exotic. Roxanne's been in the business a long time...nothing new to see there."

"You know from experience, boss?"

I winked. "My life hasn't been completely sheltered."

Sixteen

Taken in Turn

Early one morning they took Angel away and the girls never saw her again. They brought the others upstairs one by one, a few days or weeks apart. Chen wasn't sure if she should be happy or sad that she was saved until last. Listening to what happened to the other girls was terrifying, and she learned firsthand what the words rape and sex meant. Being so young, she knew she wasn't physically ready to become a woman.

When her turn came, she was surprised to see the woman from the examination room again. The food delivery boy was the only person she had seen in almost a month. The woman took her to a bedroom in another part of the house. Chen tensed and began to cry when asked to disrobe. The matron scolded her and told her to wash herself in the adjoining bathroom. Nothing fancy, it was the nicest room she'd been in since leaving home.

Chen lathered herself with the pretty-smelling soap and shampoo. The warm water was soothing and she wanted to stay in the shower forever. The woman yanked the curtain back and ordered her to towel off. Again, Chen tried to take her time, fearing what waited for her. She couldn't have been more surprised when she entered the bedroom.

A fresh set of clothes lay on the bed and a bowl of soup sat on the nightstand. The woman told her to get dressed and eat the soup. They had a long ride ahead of them and Chen wouldn't be eating again for a while. The pink skirt and blouse were a bit big, but the outfit looked pretty. The clothes were better quality than usual. The noodle soup was tasty and hot, and she had a generous chunk of bread to eat with it.

The woman answered a knock on the bedroom door. Chen saw another unknown man. She cowered and tried to become invisible, thinking it was her turn to be raped. The woman snapped at the man and closed the door. She told Chen to finish her soup and brush her hair before it dried.

The same man waited outside in a small windowless van. Chen was completely confused as to what was going on, but it was nice to fill her lungs with fresh air. She enjoyed the warmth of the sun on her face. The woman ordered her into the back of the van and they drove off, leaving the other girls behind.

Chen knew better than to ask where they were going or why the other girls weren't coming. Curtains behind the seats blocked her view out the front of the van but the slight opening between them offered a glimpse of the road and vehicles ahead. It didn't matter. Chen had no idea where she was headed.

She thought about how she missed her family. Were they looking for her and did they report her abduction to anyone? It appeared her father was responsible for her kidnapping. Maybe he paid them the money he owed, and they were returning her home. Chen was sure that wasn't the case, and feared she'd never see her family again.

They drove for hours, into the night. She fell asleep, and woke up when they stopped for gas. Chen saw nothing but darkness outside, and only heard the sound of fuel going into the tank. She liked watching her father do it and was curiously attracted to the fumes given off by the liquid he put into their vehicle. The woman stayed in the van while the man pumped. When he got back in, she parted the curtain and handed Chen a bottle of water and package of rice crackers.

It was daylight when she woke again. The van had stopped in a parking garage. Chen could tell by all the other cars and the type of building. The woman opened the side door and ordered her out of the vehicle. She squeezed her legs together and told the matron she had to pee. Her response was a nod towards a set of elevator doors. The man remained in the vehicle.

Chen had been in an elevator before but not one as fancy. Mirrored glass covered the ceiling and walls. The woman used a key to close the doors. Chen eyed her reflection and wondered what waited for her at the end of the ride. The indicator lights for the various floors flashed on and off as the lift went up.

They didn't stop until the last one, number 60. Chen had never been that high up, anywhere. The doors slid open and a mirage appeared in front of her. It couldn't be real. A grand foyer appeared, adorned with ornate columns and Chinese murals of red and gold. Chen had only seen such places in magazines at the dress shop.

A young woman in a neatly pressed uniform and apron stood in their path, holding a pair of slippers. She said nothing but motioned with her head for Chen to discard her shoes on a mat near the wall. Her new footwear was made of silk. Once she had the slippers on, the servant motioned for her to follow. Chen looked back at the old woman, but she was disappearing behind the elevator doors. It would be the last time she would ever see her. The new female in her life led her down a short hallway to a bedroom with two separate beds.

"My name is Li. This is where you stay unless you are called out to work."

She pointed to a uniform similar to hers, but smaller.

"This your bed. Remove dirty clothes, take shower, put new clothes on. I come back when you done."

The woman surprised and confused Chen. She spoke in broken English. When she left, Chen took in the room. It was the largest bedroom she had ever seen. The walls were papered with Oriental artwork, and the floor carpeted. The beds had carved headboards and beautiful linens. There were pillows. She couldn't remember the last time she laid her head on one. There was a closet filled with more uniforms like hers and Li's.

The adjoining bathroom had a marble floor and walls. Chen had never seen anything like it. She wondered why there were two toilets—one without a seat. The soap smelled even better than the one at the last house, and the shampoo came out of a device mounted on the wall. She got out of the shower and grabbed a towel. Chen thought she was in heaven. The plush cotton reminded her of the blanket she had as a child.

Seventeen

Full Plate

When I got back to the station, I popped in to see a buddy, who ran the Intelligence Unit. We spent a few minutes chewing the rag and catching up. Although we'd started on the job the same day, Shadow took a different career path and advanced to the rank of staff sergeant.

More of a company man, he made it all about fiscal responsibility when I asked to borrow a tracking device. He went on about how expensive they were and they only had one left, after someone lost the other during a surveillance operation. I countered by telling him my targets were high-end thieves who had foiled all our attempts at mobile surveillance.

My buddy finally agreed with two conditions. First, he wanted to see the tracking warrant to prove that a judge actually granted us the required permission to use the device. Second, he wanted me to help his Mobile Surveillance Unit with a special stakeout.

His team was short-handed and he knew my prior surveillance experience with both the Ontario Provincial Police and our service. He said he'd clear it with my boss so I agreed to help him out. The target was a Bank of Montreal in the Riverside area. Someone in Intelligence received information about two men who were going to rob the bank. It was supposed to happen in a few days, on a Friday, when the bank was flush with cash.

Back in my office, I sat down with King and went over the information I received from my CI about Samir Sarkis. Having arrested the man before, Mike was well aware of who he was and what he was all about. King wrote the search warrants for Project Rub n' Tug. I thought applying for a tracking warrant would be a good way for him to gain more experience.

Gelinas sat across the desk from King, and listened. I told them to spend some of their down time surveilling the area around Sarkis' apartment and the lot where he parked the vehicles he used for break-ins. Any information gleaned could be used to obtain the warrant. It was up to the police to prove why it was necessary to attach the tracking device to someone's private property.

Brian Gamble, my boss, poked his head out of his office, saw me at the back of the room talking to King and Gelinas, and asked me to see him when I was done. He trained me for two days when I was first promoted to constable, and we walked a beat downtown. That was the extent of my on-the-job training, back in the day. New recruits now spend a whole year with a training officer.

When I walked into Gamble's office, he told me to take a seat. From my side of the desk, he appeared to have aged; his hair receding and almost all grey. Maybe his nasty divorce and the two promotions had something to do with it. He was still tall dark and handsome, and always sported the typical cop mustache.

"I got your note and the investigative expense claim for a hundred dollars."

"Is that a problem, boss?"

"Maybe, you know how the bean counters are around here. I trust your judgement and your informants always seem to be solid. I'm just wondering if we can split the amount into two payments...spread it out as not to raise any eyebrows. Petty cash means exactly that to the brass, they think a hundred bucks is like a thousand."

"Whatever works for you...I'm only looking out for my informant, who's giving me info on counterfeit money and possible illegal strippers."

Gamble raised his brow. Morality, bars and strippers came under his umbrella.

"You think something fishy is going on with out-of-town peelers? It's not the first time we've gotten French girls from up north or Quebec."

"Not quite sure yet...she says they're Asian girls and the bar owner is holding their passports until they work off their debt. He's supposed to have put them up in a house somewhere. I've gotta look into it some more."

"You've got a lot on your plate, Norm. I just got off the phone with Shadow, and he says you're going to help the Intelligence guys with surveillance on a bank. I haven't seen much coming from Shorty's crew...you want me to have him step up and take more on?"

I gave Gamble my best 'are you crazy'? face.

He laughed. "Yeah...forget I asked...good thing he's got subordinates who can carry his weight. I'm just asking...heard through the grapevine, things aren't that great at home. You know I've been there if you need any advice. You have lots of vacation time saved up."

"Thanks, boss, the down time is the worst...too much to think about. I'd just hound her more and drive the wedge in deeper. I've got a good support group with family and close friends."

My boss handed me fifty bucks and put the petty cash box back in his drawer.

"Give your fink that for now and we'll square up next week. What's going on with the counterfeit bills...Fraud got any idea who's making them?"

"Not that I've heard. I've been keeping it under my hat...my brother caught his stepdaughter with a whole stack of them. She was busted in Toronto and he wants me to see what I can do. Doubt she'll say anything but it would be nice to find out where she got the funny money."

Gamble leaned back in his chair and shook his head. "You can't choose your family...good luck with that. And like I said, Norm, you need anything, you let me know."

I got up and stuffed the fifty bucks in my pocket.

"I will. Thanks."

Eighteen

T-Bone Steak-Out

JP handled the briefing in the closet-sized office. He was in charge of our Spin Team (Mobile Surveillance Unit) and my former roommate when I first got on the job. The MSU really didn't need much of an office because most of their job took place on the road; conducting static and mobile surveillance on pre-selected targets. Their targets could be anyone, from shoplifters to murder suspects.

My old roomy was the team leader, a Sergeant, who also worked in the unit before his promotion. Surveillance was an acquired art, and JP was good at it. At full strength, the unit consisted of five members, all of whom worked in plain clothes, and used different types of unmarked vehicles, parked off-site when they weren't working.

Fulfilling my promise to Shadow, who was JP's brother-in-law, I replaced one of the Spin Team members who was off work with an injury. Where static or stationary surveillance was usually boring, being on the move during a mobile spin was much more fun. The idea was to follow or track the target without being burned (compromised).

In many cases, it was much easier said than done. During my assignment with the OPP Spin Team, I learned some invaluable lessons. The first was to stick to your post—plug in and stay put unless the target is on the move. For the OPP gig, we followed a known B & E boy in the Town of Belle River. The target was especially hard to follow because he used his bicycle to prowl residential streets, looking for houses to break into. The suspect resided in the outskirts of town on a dead-end street, leaving him only one route into town.

The officer who had 'the eye' on the target's home radioed he was on the move, riding his bicycle in my direction. I stood out like the last ball on a pool table, being the only car parked on the country road. Acting quickly, I grabbed my clipboard and headed to the house under construction behind me.

I struck up a conversation with two men who were working on the foundation. Out of the corner of my eye, I saw the target stop and check out my car. He looked through the windows, and eyeballed me for what seemed like forever. I assumed my ruse worked when he rode off.

A short time later, the target stopped and went into a variety store in town. The team plugged in, covering three, six, nine and twelve—the east, south, west and north sides—boxing him in. The team leader said he had the eye but I saw him drive by the store at least three times. On the third pass, the dirt bag stepped out of the store and took pictures of our leader with a disposable camera he purchased inside. Lesson learned, never drive by more than once.

JP handed me mug shots of the two suspects who he believed were going to rob the Bank of Montreal at Wyandotte and Watson. I had heard one of the names before, but didn't recognize either of the men. They both had lengthy records for a variety of crimes; some included the use of weapons. It wasn't something I normally did in plain clothes, but I wore my bulletproof vest that day.

We were set up before the bank opened, not knowing exactly when the suspects planned to do the job. The bank was at a busy intersection, with four possible escape routes. Our team had all four directions covered, and a marked police cruiser hidden about two blocks away. JP started with the eye, letting us know when the business opened its doors. In the next hour, he called out two suspicious-looking vehicles; we had no idea what the bad guys were driving.

Having done surveillance before, I came prepared. An egg McMuffin from MacDonald's was my breakfast, something I ate as soon as we set up. Lunch and various snacks were in my duffle bag, along with binoculars and a jacket and ballcap, to change my appearance when necessary. For a Friday, business seemed slow at the bank. About a half hour before noon, JP called for a bathroom break, and told us to switch places before the lunchtime rush.

Various takedown scenarios played in my mind. There were more ways than one to arrest armed suspects who were about to rob a bank. Optimally, the tactical team would do it but they were out of town at training camp. The safety of everyone involved is the main concern. The difficulty we faced was in identifying the suspects before they got into the bank and robbed it.

It would seem simpler to let them rob the place and follow them to a safe location where we could arrest them without incident. No matter how good the plan, more often than not, something goes wrong. I saw it many times during raids when I worked in the Drug Squad. Leaving my position, I went to relieve JP. The route took me past the front of the bank, where traffic was backed up.

A car turned left in front of me and pulled into the no parking zone on the southwest corner of the intersection. I had a clear view of the passenger in the black Impala. He was staring at the front door of the bank, and he had a sawed-off rifle in his hands. I didn't recognize him from the photos but there was no doubt in my mind he was about to rob the bank.

Traffic prohibited me from turning in behind the Impala but I notified the others by radio. JP had seen me coming and was already vacating his spot to make room for my car. My foot was on the brake while I watched the suspect vehicle in the mirrors. JP took advantage of the gap I left in front of me and turned left across my lane. He made a beeline for the Impala and T-boned the driver's side, effectively pinning him inside.

The passenger had been on his way out of the car and the impact sent him sprawling onto the sidewalk. By the time he regained his senses, the cop who was covering southbound Watson had him at gunpoint. The driver didn't know what hit him and lost his handgun under the front seat. JP had no problem affecting the arrest. Both men were taken into custody without further incident. Not quite a textbook takedown, but it worked.

In all the confusion after the arrests, I couldn't find my old roomy. He had run into the bank to tell them everything was okay, and that he needed their bathroom. The bad news was we couldn't charge the two men with robbery since they didn't complete the act. The good news was we were able to charge them with attempted robbery and enough weapons charges that would keep them locked up for a while.

Nineteen

Learning the Ropes

For the next six months Li taught Chen her job; how to be the perfect housekeeper and more. It was clear to her that Mr. and Mrs. Wong were her masters, and she was to take care of their every need if she wanted to remain in their home and not end up on the street. Chen wasn't exactly sure what on the street meant. It didn't matter how fancy the Wong household was, she'd rather be back in her own home.

The rich strangers could never replace her family, even though Mr. Wong was very nice to her when he was home. Mrs. Wong was an angry woman, who spent most of the day in her own wing of the penthouse apartment. The only time Chen saw the couple together was at dinner when Mr. Wong wasn't away on business.

Li had told her that Mr. Wong owned several businesses in China and even a few in the United States and Canada, but she had no idea what he did. Li became the big sister Chen never had. They grew close, but the young woman never revealed much about her personal life. Thinking Li was much older, Chen was shocked to find out she was only sixteen.

It seemed her mentor was keeping something secret. Like where she disappeared to every second or third night. Li quietly slipped out of their bedroom after she thought her roommate was asleep. She always returned within a half hour and sometimes cried herself to sleep. Chen once asked where she went at night, but Li only said she'd explain when Chen was older.

That day came a week later when her only friend in the world said she was leaving. Li told her she would be in charge of running the house. She told Chen to pay special attention to Mr. Wong's requests. Her mentor expressed how important it was to please her master if she wished to stay off the street.

Chen was upset Li was leaving, and asked why and where she was going. Her friend said she had no idea, it wasn't up to her, and Mr. Wong's business associates would be coming to pick her up. Chen had so many more questions about Mr. Wong. Li told her he would come to her and she should be nice to him. Her well-being would depend on it.

Li cried most of that night and disappeared the next morning. Mrs. Wong never said a word, offering only a scowl as her housekeeper was whisked away. Her husband was away on business. She glared at Chen as soon as the door closed, and demanded her morning tea in her sitting room.

It was almost a week later, when Mr. Wong returned home. It was late when he knocked on Chen's bedroom door. She let him in. He was more affectionate than usual and he told her she was beautiful. Wong went on about how he missed her, and at one point put a hand on her shoulder.

Li's parting advice whipped through her head but she was confused.

Her master sat beside her on the bed and put his arm around her. Chen tensed as his hand slid down her back to her buttocks. He reached around and caressed her thigh, letting his fingers slip under her nightie. Before she could move away, he pushed her back onto the bed. She tried to scream but Wong put his hand over her mouth and told her to keep quiet.

Chen wasn't sure what happened next but presumed it was rape. It was her turn. She had considered herself lucky it didn't happen before, and now understood the pain it caused the other girls. What Mr. Wong did to her that night was a blur. It really hurt and she didn't understand why he did it. She thought sex was something shared between a husband and wife, and his was just down the hall.

It all made sense now. She suddenly understood where Li had disappeared to at night and why she came back in tears. It was not the joyful experience she thought sex was supposed to be. Chen felt used. When Wong finished with her, he simply got up and left her bedroom. Was she to be Li's replacement? Her life had suddenly taken a turn for the worse.

Twenty

Pizza & Beer

Something you never really see on police shows or in the movies is cops doing paperwork. The reason being it is boring and takes hours upon hours to complete. In the case of the takedown at the bank, five police officers were taken off the street to complete surveillance and supplementary reports, arrest reports, use of force reports, and an accident report.

Granted, computerization made things easier for someone like me who learned how to type in high school, but it was very time-consuming for those who could only use two fingers. It was definitely better than when I first got on the job and had to write or type everything in triplicate, using carbon paper to make copies.

Completing the paperwork got us some overtime and we didn't wrap everything up until it was past time for dinner. Although no special accolades came down the pipe from higher up, we thought our success was worthy of pizza and beer at a local watering hole that catered to cops. Eating and drinking was something I enjoyed, the latter more so since my trouble at home.

I had a three-day weekend. Under normal circumstance, I would have enjoyed getting out of the city and away from my job. But my life wasn't normal anymore. In fact, I had no idea what lay ahead for me, and my marriage. It all seemed beyond my control. The more I pushed my wife for answers, the further away she drifted. I couldn't keep my investigative cop instincts under control.

My pond and back yard offered me solace. I deadheaded some of the perennials and netted the pond to keep out falling leaves. The fish moved in slow motion, adjusting to the change in water temperature. Frogs, even Fat Frank, were disappearing and finding shelter for the season ahead. Hues of red and orange foliage confirmed autumn had a firm grip on my little piece of paradise.

Bent over and fiddling with the net, I heard a familiar sound behind me. My vast experience in deciphering different tones told me it was the clinking of beer bottles. I turned to see my brother Willy standing on the deck, holding two coolies. My back reminded me of an old injury when I stood up, and I worked my palms into the aching muscles surrounding the afflicted area.

"You look thirsty, bro, time for a break."

Where my father and two brothers liked to have beer breaks between household chores, it wasn't a habit of mine. There are exceptions to every rule, and socially imbibing with company was one of them.

"Little brother...where's your better half?"

"At mom's, discussing the Lisa situation. I thought maybe the drill sergeant, could offer her some advice. Glad she's not my daughter...maybe I should be more like mom when we were kids and get the paddle out."

"Worked on me…kinda…just thinking about that thing makes me cringe."

We pulled out two chairs away from the table on the deck and turned them to face the pond. Willy had put in a smaller version at his place, and adopted some of my fish.

"What's the latest on Lisa?"

"She's back home…just showed up like she'd only been gone overnight. Didn't say a word about being arrested until we brought it up. She told us she had it under control—whatever that's supposed to mean."

"Where's the boyfriend?"

"Don't know. Sharlene's sister said the cops questioned her when she bailed Lisa out…wanted to know where he was. Guess he split when she got busted."

"Nice guy."

"Yeah, seems to be the kind she's attracted to…bad boys. Were you able to reach out to the cops up in Toronto?"

I took a pull off my bottle of beer and shook my head.

"No, but I requested a copy of their reports to see what we're dealing with. I'd rather talk to her first, and see what she has to offer, or if she even wants to help herself out."

"I don't know about that…she doesn't say shit to us. Guess she's got it all figured out."

Willy reached for his beer. "How you doing? Heard you're having woman problems too…she in the house?"

"No, she's out." I dropped my eyes to my lap. "Thought I had a good marriage…shows you never really know someone as well as you think."

"Are you working things out?"

"I have no fucking idea."

Sharlene came around the back corner of the house. By the look of her mascara, I could tell she'd been crying.

"Hey, Norm, got any wine?"

Twenty-One

Roll Over Beethoven

Some might say cultivating confidential informants is an art in itself. I didn't consider myself artistic in that regard, but I learned a lot of what to do, and what not to do, when I was in the Drug Squad. I watched other officers arrest drug dealers, treat them like dog shit they'd just stepped in, and try to roll them over to give up information on another dealer.

I truly believed in something my mom used to say when I was a kid—how you catch more flies with honey. It didn't take a psychologist to figure out why someone didn't want to talk, after being treated like shit. Granted, they may have been a criminal, and a drug dealer, but they were human beings with feelings.

Even when I worked in uniform, my philosophy was to treat people the way I wanted to be treated. A little respect goes a long way. It saved me from a lot of fighting on the street, and it got me confidential informants. Nobody wants to be a rat. People supply the police with information for many reasons, but if they can help themselves by helping the police, and you offer them a bit of honey, they usually drink the tea.

It was comical when I tried to bring my boss in Street Crimes up to speed on things. I said my *buddy* (no names unless necessary) told me blah, blah, blah, about this and that. He said, 'the guy who told you about the massage parlor'? I said, 'no the guy who told me about the other thing'. Then he asked how many informants I had. Truth was I never really counted.

A few of my CIs stayed in touch. Others only called when they wanted something. There were some I reached out to, if I thought they might be able to help me with a particular investigation. They were people who had their own lives. Some moved on and others never changed. It was the way of the world.

Normally on Sunday mornings, I made myself a big breakfast. Eating was one of my favorite pastimes and breakfast was my favorite meal of the day. My wife did her best to avoid me because I was doing my best to get in her face, trying to get answers why.

After getting my bacon fix, I called Willy to see if Lisa was home. He said she was and I told him to keep her corralled, that I'd be over in a bit to have a sit-down with her. That was fine by him, she hadn't said much to them since she'd returned home. He told me the boyfriend hadn't been around either, and suspected they had a fight, or he thought she was a heat score after getting busted.

When I got to my brother's place, he was raking leaves. Willy was pissed off because he didn't have any trees on his property and all the leaves came from the neighbors. He told me Lisa was watching TV in the basement. I said a brief hello to Sharlene on the way through the kitchen, and went downstairs.

Lisa gave me a casual glance but turned her attention back to the television. She knew why I was there. I grabbed the remote and shut the TV off. That got her attention and she gave me a pissy look.

"I ain't no rat, and my lawyer says that it's my first offence...he can probably get me probation."

I sat down in the chair facing her and stuffed the TV remote under the pillow beside me. Lisa was an attractive girl with long blonde hair and brown eyes. She was thin but shapely, with pasty-white skin and a few tattoos.

"By lawyer, you mean the public defender who showed up in arraignment court with you and by probation, he means if you're lucky. You'll still have a criminal record that will screw up your chances of ever landing a decent job."

"Whatever. I don't need another lecture, if that's what you're here for."

"Nope...just a reality check. I'm not one to throw stones...I did my share of stupid things before I became a cop. If I hadn't joined up, I'd probably be in your shoes, or worse."

Lisa made eye contact with me for the first time.

"Like what, throwing eggs at the neighbor's house, or knocking on their doors and running away...I've heard those stories growing up."

I scoffed. "Yeah, I did those things...along with stealing beer from the neighbor's garage, bread from the grocery store, chocolate bars from the variety store, fishing tackle from Crappy Tire, and I even sold a few nickel bags of weed to my friends."

Her eyes grew large and she stared as if she didn't know me.

"Bullshit...you're just saying those things to make me rat out my friends. I know how cops work."

"Call my brother down here and ask him—he knows some of the things I did before I got on the job. Your friends, huh...where are they now? Where's the boyfriend?"

"He's an asshole, took off when the cops came. Always said he'd take care of me if something happened. Haven't heard shit from him and he changed his number. My friends say he's laying low, already thinks I talked to the cops."

I could see she was pissed off at the boyfriend and decided to work that angle.

"There you go...he thinks you already ratted him out. Doesn't matter that you didn't—you're the plague now and he's going to avoid you at all costs. It's obvious he doesn't give a shit about you. But your parents do and so do I."

"You just want me to help you bust my friends so you can look good."

"Honestly, Lisa, chances are they will get busted with or without your help. Sooner or later they all go down. I read the Toronto file...they know who your boyfriend is and will be looking for him. It wasn't his first time. He's got quite the record."

"So what? Even if I helped you find him, it wasn't his money. He buys the fake bills from another guy, and we drive around and spend it. I have no idea who the guy is."

I slid forward in my seat and rested my elbows on my knees.

"Let me tell you how you can get out of this mess...how I might be able to help."

She'd taken on a bit of a pouty face but stayed quiet and listened. I went on to tell her how the game was really played behind the scenes. Even hardened criminals, who say they'd never rat on anyone, take care of number one. It was true, I knew from personal experience. A seasoned detective once came to me in the Drug Squad with an informant who wanted out of an arrest warrant and was willing to trade information.

That's when I learned how to read a criminal record card, not knowing before how someone like him could have so many charges withdrawn or dismissed. He knew how to play the game. Without giving his name, I used the biker as an example to drive home my point. Her pout turned into more of an inquisitive expression. She nibbled on the bait.

"So, what would I have to do to stay out of jail? I don't care about having a record but I can't stand the thought of being locked up in a cage."

"Information, Lisa. It makes the world go around. In my work, cops in Toronto are the same as cops here—our job is to lock up bad guys. Getting information from informants makes it a lot easier. Those informants are rewarded in different ways. Some do it for cash and others like you, trade information for leniency or forgiveness regarding their criminal charges. It's a win-win for the good and bad guys."

She pulled her legs up off the floor and folded them under her. Leaning forward, with her arms crossed over her knees, she stared into the empty space behind me. Seeing she was thinking, I kept my mouth shut and waited.

"Billy, my ex-boyfriend, who you're looking for, has always been an asshole and treated me like shit. I stuck around for the money and drugs. He took me to great parties and let me keep some of the stuff we bought with the phony money."

I really didn't want to know if she still had any of the contraband. I let her go on.

"He always had party material and knew where to buy weed and coke. I don't know where he got the fake hundreds, but we partied at his weed dealer's house once. The guy had a bunch of plants growing in an old greenhouse out back of his place."

There it was. She was catching on. I sat back in my chair and asked her to tell me more.

Twenty-Two

Used and Abused

Mr. Wong was usually gentle with Chen, except for the fact he was forcing himself on her. His visits to her bedroom were almost nightly at first. She wondered how Mrs. Wong could not know what was going on in her own house...or did she? Chen thought the act of copulation between husband and wife was called making love. Since there was no love between her and her master, it was simply rape.

Wong was average in height and weight, compared to other Asian men. Chen thought he was about her father's age. He always dressed well, even at home, and he smelled good; the perfect gentleman outside of her bedroom. Once in her room, his grunting, groaning, and sweating, reminded her of a farm animal.

Chen took no pleasure in what Mr. Wong did to her. It caused her pain at times and Wong was aware of it. When she showed discomfort, he only got more excited. She bled the first time he molested her. She thought it had something to do with what her mother had taught her about women's bodies, and what happened when they came of age.

When she bled heavily one night during intercourse with Wong, he became disgusted with her and said she should have warned him about her period. Chen thought she knew what to do. She caught Li tending to herself in the bathroom one day. Li left some personal supplies there and Chen was able to control her bleeding.

It was if Wong knew more about her body than she did. He resumed his ritual right on schedule, not mentioning the previous incident. There was limited conversation during his visits to her bedroom. It was as if she was only a receptacle for his seed. He sometimes said something flattering to gain her favor, as if it would make a difference in what was about to happen. What could she possibly have to say to a man who was physically abusing her almost every night?

Chen's household cleaning duties took her into Wong's office at times, and she heard parts of his business conversations on the phone. He paid no attention to her when she was outside of her bedroom. Chen had no idea what type of business her master was in but heard him speak of shipments or packages sent overseas.

On one occasion, he scolded the person on the other end of the phone about damaged goods, and how much money it cost him to replace them. Wong said he expected compensation with quality merchandise, and might sample one item himself to test the product. Chen heard similar conversations but didn't know what he was talking about.

Mrs. Wong never had a kind word for Chen, and on one occasion while changing the linen in her bedroom, the woman called her *jinu*, which meant prostitute in her language. Chen had no idea how to respond, or tell the woman her husband was raping her and she had no choice in the matter. She put her head down and left the room. Chen didn't know if it was a good or bad thing Mrs. Wong knew what was going on.

Twenty-Three

Wheels in Motion

Back at work, I dealt with the morning ritual of sorting through paperwork on any overnight arrests and break-in reports. There weren't many follow-ups to assign but two custodies would keep my crew busy until at least lunchtime. I thought about my conversation with my step-niece, Lisa. Admittedly, I was a bit surprised she decided to talk.

At my request, she gave me the names of people in her circle, obviously not telling me about all of them. Nobody likes to give up all their dealers. I was particularly interested in the guy growing weed and anyone else at his house party. She remembered someone she thought was cute, a blonde pretty-boy who drove a red muscle car. She didn't know the make, but it was a convertible. He had a bimbo with him. She couldn't remember her name but his was Jeff.

It's funny the things you remember. I had a good memory for names and an even better one for faces; a good thing to have in my line of work. When I was in the drug squad, I busted a guy by the name of Joffe Watson, and he became a CI to work his patch. He drove a candy apple red Ford Mustang convertible, and had a bleached-blonde girlfriend who could easily fit the bimbo description.

Checking the clock, I took a break from my paperwork. It wasn't going anywhere and I wanted to check next door in the Drug Squad to see if Tina Farmer was working. She transferred to Drugs when I was on my way out so I handed off Joffe to her. It made more sense for her to be his handler. Drug info wouldn't do me any good in Street Crimes.

Farmer was getting dressed for court when I walked into the Drug office. She said Joffe gave her one bust but he was still on the hook for his outstanding charges. I caught him with weed and a gun. After listening to me repeat all of Lisa's information on the weed dealer with the grow-op, Tina said she'd give Joffe a call after court and look into it.

My buddy, Blackjack, caught me on the way out and suggested breakfast. He didn't have to ask me twice. Any work we had to do would still be there when we got back. We went to our favorite downtown deli. Cops were allowed to walk in the back door. Elias Deli was a Windsor fixture offering the best corned beef hash I ever had. I always worked better on a full stomach.

King and Gelinas were busy most of the day and it wasn't until mid-afternoon when Mike pulled up a chair beside my desk. He produced a rough draft of the tracking warrant he'd been working on, and he brought me up to speed on the surveillance they did on Samir Sarkis. They hadn't seen much around the apartment and he wondered if I'd heard anymore from my informant.

It was a bit odd I hadn't heard from Ham in almost a week so I told King I'd call him and check in. While saying that, I wondered if it wouldn't be a better idea to hook the two of them up directly so I didn't have to be a go-between.

With my mind constantly fretting over my marital status, it seemed the more prudent thing to do. I asked Mike if he had a problem with that.

"He's your CI, boss, if you're okay with it..."

"I'm fine with it, and I've got lots of other things going on right now. Besides, you could use the experience in dealing with an informant—have you ever had one?"

"No, I spent too much time in Traffic Enforcement, handing out tickets. Not a good environment for cultivating informants."

"I'll run it by Ham, he probably won't care. Then you can deal with his calls at all hours of the day and night."

"Thanks. I think."

I took his warrant application from him and told him to grab Gelinas and hit the road, get a jump on traffic. She heard me, locked up her desk, and was almost to the door when King caught up to her. Those two were like my left and right hands. They would make great detectives some-day.

The Auto Squad and my boss had already checked out for the day, leaving me all alone in the office. Picking up King's tracking warrant from my desk I pulled out my lower drawer, leaned back in my chair, and put my feet up. The peace and quiet was nice. No phones ringing, and nobody bothering me. Being in no particular hurry to get home, I read over the application for a tracking warrant.

I'd managed to make it to the last line, when my phone broke the silence. It was Tina Farmer. She talked to Joffe and he gave her the name of Warren Willis. He had a large forced grow operation in the old greenhouse at the back of his property. I had never heard of the guy, but that didn't mean anything. She checked it out herself and confirmed the address, but said she couldn't get to the greenhouse without going on his property.

"Sounds like you need a sneak and peek." I offered.

"A sneaky Pete?"

I laughed. "No…a sneak and peek…a general warrant…"

There was silence on the other end of the phone.

"Sorry, Storm…I don't know what you mean."

"A criminal code general warrant that allows you to check the property…like to look over a fence or enter a gated area to gather evidence to further your search…ask your boss about it when you get back in. It's about time you learn how to do one."

I could hear her trying to explain what I said to whoever was in the car with her. Farmer said she'd get right on it since it was late in the season, and the guy could be harvesting any time. I agreed and told her to keep me in the loop. She ended the call.

After reading King's warrant, I attached a sticky-note with a smiley face to the front page, walked it to the front of the office, and slipped it into his mailbox. A window on the north side of the building offered a partial view of the Detroit River and some of the high rises on the other side of the border. Seeing the sun so low in the western sky at that time of day was another sign of the harvest season.

I watched a lake freighter heading upstream to who-knows-where, and wondered if I would be able to salvage my marriage. My wife wasn't saying or doing much to convince me it was a two-way effort. A stomach growl reminded me it was time to eat, and I thought my cat and dog probably felt the same way. Time to call it a day.

Twenty-Four

Time

I heard time went by faster as you got older. That surely seemed to be the case when I was busy at work. Twenty-four years on the job had flown by, most of it a blur. At that stage of the game, it was time to think about winding down and preparing for retirement. Even though I liked being busy, and mostly enjoyed my job, I'd been planning the end of my career since the day I started it.

Another week virtually disappeared from the calendar. King got his tracking warrant, acting on information from my CI, Ham. Mike and Kristen spent most of their evenings waiting and watching for Samir Sarkis to go on the prowl. They'd seen him driving an older Ford Crown Victoria and attached the tracking device after he parked it for the night. It was only a matter of time before he went on the move again.

We used to call it the Friday Night Fights prior to 911. Thousands of underage Americans flooded the Windsor bars in search of high-test Canadian beer and spirits. Things changed drastically after they tightened the border, and the Yanks stayed home. Between the bars and the bingos, the city's population grew by about twenty thousand on the weekends. It meant job security for us cops.

There was never any shortage of work since I'd been on the job, and I found it only got busier as time went on. Driving around solo, I checked in with my crew on the radio and drove the strip, downtown. I was going nowhere in particular, when Roxanne called me and asked if I had time for a coffee. With nothing better to do, I agreed to meet her at the Tim Horton's closest to her club. She said she was working and needed a break.

I pulled into a parking spot facing the strip club and watched for Roxanne. There was a tap on my passenger window before I put the car into park. She jumped in when I unlocked the door.

"Hey Storm, can you wheel me into the drive through?"

I complied and turned to her when the attendant asked for our order. Roxanne asked for a cup of hot water and nothing else. Somewhat surprised, I ordered a diet Pepsi and chocolate chunk cookie. Before I could ask, Roxanne complained about a group of rowdy Americans that were driving her crazy.

"I had to get out of there...you'd think those kids never saw a naked woman before...they grope you anytime you're within arm's reach and actually try to bargain for lap dances—like they're afraid to spend their allowance. I hate dealing with those little fuckers."

Roxanne was wound tighter than a jack-in-the-box. The drive through attendant handed me our order, sporting a look on her face that said, 'what on earth is the hot water for'? I searched for a dark corner of the parking lot and shut off the car. Roxanne had already pulled a little bag out of her purse. It contained her kit. She asked me if I had a newer ten or twenty-dollar bill.

"You don't mind if I fix, do ya, Storm, I gotta calm down if I'm gonna make it through the night."

I already had my lips wrapped around my cookie and offered a shrug. A sugar high was enough for me. She prepared her spoon and needle, and pulled the cotton filter from a cigarette. She crushed a pill with the double sawbuck I gave her. When she held out her arm to tie it off, her coat came open.

The view stole my attention from what she was doing to her arm. Her breasts bulged from a black lace bra. She wore the matching skimpy thong. One thigh was visible, partially covered by a garter and black fishnet stocking. The ensemble paired perfectly with her short coal-black hair and steel-blue eyes.

Roxanne injected Dilaudid into her vein. I was amazed at how fast she reacted and calmed down. It was as if someone turned off a switch inside her. She caught me ogling her and closed her open coat.

"What, you're shy now?"

"No...this is different, Storm, and you're married, aren't you?"

"Not at the moment."

"Yeah, like I haven't heard that one before." She caught something in my eyes. "You're serious, aren't you? Trouble at home?"

"You could say that...I don't want to talk about it. Anyway, did you call me just to get high or is there something else?"

Roxanne lifted her chin to the motel at the other end of the plaza.

"Some of the new Asian girls they brought in are turning tricks...you should watch that place one night and see what's going on. They hook up in the club and then disappear for an hour while they come over here to meet their johns."

"Cutting into your business?"

I knew I shouldn't have said it as soon as the words left my lips. Roxanne gave me the stink-eye, as if I just grabbed her by the crotch. She opened her door to get out, and tossed the cup of water.

"Fuck you, Storm...you know I don't do that."

"I'm sorry...I'm sorry, I didn't mean it."

She got out of my car, taking the twenty with her. I didn't have the heart to ask for it back. She turned back to me for a second before shutting the door.

"You still owe me fifty."

She winked and shot me a sly smirk, before walking away. I sat there thinking about her for a minute while I finished my pop. My thoughts wandered to Sandra and what was or wasn't going on between us. I hated drama and it really bothered me how it had crept into my life. Crumpling the empty pop cup and paper bag, I searched for a garbage can in the area.

My radio came to life, and King told me Samir Sarkis was on the move.

Twenty-Five

Happy Birthday

Chen checked the kitchen calendar for two reasons. First, she wanted to keep track of how long she was in captivity. Second, her fourteenth birthday was a week away. She debated whether she should mark the calendar in the hope the Wong's would do something nice for her special day. It was something to wish for.

The day before her birthday Mr. Wong told her to pack her bag. He was going on a business trip and she was to accompany him. Chen's face lit up with excitement and she thanked her master for the early gift. Not knowing what she was talking about, he shrugged and walked away.

That night during dinner, the Wong's got into a heated argument. Chen always ate in her bedroom but she heard their voices echoing down the main hallway. Mrs. Wong was unhappy about having to break in a new maid, and downright angry she had no say in choosing a replacement. Chen wondered exactly how long she and Mr. Wong would be away. He told her nothing.

The next morning, on her birthday, a familiar face stepped off the elevator and into the foyer. It was the same

Asian woman, who brought her there. Chen thought it odd to see her after all that time. She tilted her head toward the open doors and said, 'you come now.' Mr. Wong patted his young slave on the back and told her to go on ahead. He'd catch up with them later.

The elevator brought Chen to the parking garage she hadn't seen since being delivered to the Wong's. A windowless van similar to the one she came in was waiting for them. The vehicle's driver was a different man. Emotions Chen hadn't experienced in a while started to creep up on her. Something didn't feel right. A knot formed in her stomach and fear began to course through her veins.

She asked the woman when they'd be meeting Mr. Wong and she responded by handing Chen a bottle of water. Already nervous, and dehydrated, she took a long drink. All kinds of thoughts ran through her head. Where was she going now? Was she really meeting up with Mr. Wong? Did he lie to her? Did she do something wrong? Was she being punished...or being sent back to the basement, where she was held with the other girls?

The thoughts were tiring and Chen felt drowsy. She wanted to ask the woman more questions but her eyes and limbs grew so heavy she had to lay down. When she woke up, Chen was in another strange room. She was groggy and felt like she'd slept for days. There was nobody else around.

Chen tried to focus and take in the room but her vision was a bit fuzzy. She was in a bed and felt dizzy when she sat up. She reached for a bottle of water on the table beside her but stopped short of grasping it, remembering how the last drink made her feel. All of a sudden, Chen was scared again. What were these people doing and where had they taken her?

Now, more than ever before, the young girl wished for home.

Twenty-Six

Follow the Leader

King and Gelinas operated on our private channel, not monitored by dispatcher, so I told him I'd call in for uniform assistance. Sarkis lived in the west end and according to the tracking device; he was heading south from Tecumseh Road. My gut told me he would return to the same subdivision where we busted him before, probably for unfinished business. King said the tracker was working well and they were staying out of sight.

The dispatcher was able to give me the #3 district car and I told her to have them switch one of their radios to our channel. She said another car should be available soon and she would send them my way. Broadcasting over the main city channel wasn't a good idea for various reasons, the most important being the bad guys might pick us up on their scanners. The channel also had lots of air traffic. I knew from experience; this would muck things up.

When King announced Sarkis was southbound on Howard, I was sure he was headed for Southwood Lakes. In anticipation, I had the district car meet me at a nearby mall parking lot. King continued to give me the play by play while I met with the uniforms and filled them in. He was concerned when Samir turned into Southwood Lakes, knowing it would be too easy for us to be burned trying to follow him.

Traffic was virtually non-existent in the neighborhood at that time of night so I understood perfectly. He asked how they would know which house the target was breaking into, if they weren't close enough to witness it. It was a good question. The most difficult part of conducting surveillance is not being compromised. I suggested one of them go in on foot but King said he was unsure of how accurate the tracker was.

There were only three entrances and exits from the subdivision so I told him to stay and watch the main one on Howard. I sent the uniform car to the exit further south on Howard and I took the one on North Talbot. King continued to call out Samir's movements, saying he had circled back twice, probably doing heat checks, and stopped on Suncrest. He wasn't sure of the block number but took note of the cross streets.

Waiting for someone to commit a particular crime, and playing out the take down and arrest in your head, is nerve-racking. Patrol officers were used to roaring up to a crime in progress and asked if they shouldn't be going in. I told them to be patient and stay put. It wouldn't seem right to an outsider, letting the crime take place, but it was the best way to catch them red-handed, after they actually committed a criminal offence.

We waited. The silence was deafening, until the dispatcher startled me, asking for an update. I told her to stand by and asked about the other patrol car. She said they should be clear shortly. That sounded familiar. King said they were on the move, and I felt my butt cheeks tighten. Staring into the darkness, I kept a keen eye for the old Crown Vic, wondering if they'd come my way.

My grip on the steering wheel tightened when King reported they were heading in my direction. But Sarkis looped back around, drove another circle, and stopped again, deeper into the subdivision. King asked what to do.

"They're gonna hit another place. Hang tight. You copy that 103?"

"10-4, we're standing by."

We waited some more. The worst part was thinking, wondering, guessing, and second-guessing. The whole idea was to stop and arrest Sarkis before he got out onto the open road. High-speed chases were mostly illegal, especially if you knew who was behind the wheel. We couldn't let him by us with evidence in hand. The next ten minutes seemed like an hour.

"They're on the move again, Storm, heading out the main exit right towards us. We've got the road blocked with our car."

I moved my vehicle across the exit and considered the decorative ponds on both sides of the road. They would get wet if they tried to drive around me. I could hear the excitement in King's voice. He was monitoring the tracker and told Gelinas to move the car tighter to the curb. It was official. Sarkis headed towards their exit. Upon seeing the unmarked car blocking his path, Sarkis accelerated and headed straight for it.

Not sure what to do, Gelinas grabbed the gear shift, and put her foot over the accelerator. Before she could make a decision, the Crown Vic jumped the curb, and drove over the grass between the subdivision sign and a stand of pine trees. The car clipped the sign, damaging the left side. King called out the action, confirming Samir was driving and fled north on Howard like a wounded deer.

I knew exactly what would happen next if I didn't say something—everyone would fall in behind and the chase would be on. The dispatcher would tell us to use caution. The Patrol Staff Sergeant would tell us to call off the chase. I beat everyone to the punch and told the team to give Sarkis some rope.

"Mike, you and Kristen take a few deep breaths, you can check your pants later. Get your eyes back on the tracker, and call him out again. Let him think he got away. We'll regroup and catch up with him later. Copy that, 103?"

They acknowledged and I told them to parallel us on Dougal Road as long as the target stayed on Howard. According to King, Sarkis left Howard at the railway tracks and ducked in behind a plaza off West Grand and Dougal, where he stopped the car. Again, we kept our distance but kept him boxed. I asked the dispatcher not to mention us, or the suspect vehicle on the open channel.

About ten minutes later, the target headed south on Dougal and west on South Cameron. He was taking the back roads home.

"He's headed for the nest, guys. Unit 103, you're in a good position...can you race down Huron Church and get in behind his apartment building? Sit in the shadows and wait for him there. We'll try to follow and block him in."

They acknowledged and I caught up to King and Gelinas. I stayed on their six. We now had a plan B and I really hoped it worked this time. Sarkis was almost home, and was probably feeling confident he'd pulled it off. About three blocks from home, he did another heat check, making a series of right turns that eventually put him on his own street. He stopped a block short of his place, probably to take one more look.

As he pulled into the laneway of his parking lot, King and Gelinas, and I raced to catch up.

When he spotted the police cruiser, it was too late. Gelinas accelerated to block him in. Sarkis had nowhere to go. He made a last-ditch attempt to get around their car, but wedged the Crown Vic in between it and his apartment building.

The patrol officers were on the bandits before the car came to rest. I was in the second car back and looked on as if watching an episode of Cops. It was hard to remember when I could move as fast as those two young policemen. They cuffed the culprits and called for the paddy wagon. King and Gelinas checked the trunk of the Crown Victoria and found it full of stolen jewelry and electronics.

Leaving my crew to collect the evidence I went back to Southwood Lakes and met up with another patrol car. Using the information King gave me, we located the two burglarized homes. None of the occupants from either location were home. I left the uniforms to handle the break-in reports and headed back to the cop shop to help with the paperwork.

The team effort resulted in a good bust, and a slew of criminal charges. Ham might be disappointed he wouldn't be getting any of the stolen jewelry, but I knew he'd be happy with the cash reward he'd receive instead. I took satisfaction in knowing Samir Sarkis would be heading back to jail a lot sooner than he planned.

Twenty-Seven

One Bad Apple

One day off just wasn't enough. I returned to work to find police investigators had searched my desk, and arrested one of my coworkers. I shared the desk with the detective, who worked the shift opposite to me, but we each had our own set of locked drawers. As it turned out, they found a stolen iPad in one of his section of the desk. The arrest shocked everyone in our office.

We all knew there was an ongoing investigation into lumber stolen from a private business. A pickup truck, the suspect vehicle, was one of our fleet, and used by various plain clothed officers, including myself. I was called into the Inspector's office about a month earlier, and questioned in regard to the dates I signed out that truck.

Thinking about the dates and checking my notes for the vehicles I signed out, I couldn't help but think about the time I used that same pickup truck during a series of drug raids on marijuana grow operations. We filled the back of the vehicle with green garbage bags full of confiscated plants and I drove them to the police station. On route, the dispatcher asked me what kind of truck I was driving.

Apparently, a citizen called in to report a man driving around the city with a truck full of weed. That was funny, but questions about the same truck and stolen lumber were not. I couldn't imagine another cop being stupid enough to do that, but someone might have thought the same about me with the weed.

Soon after the arrest, I heard rumors I was the rat who gave up one of my fellow officers; coincidentally a man of the same rank who shared my desk. It didn't seem to matter I didn't have access to his locked drawers or he had signed out the vehicle and stole the lumber. They charged the detective with theft and possession, and later demoted him upon conviction.

In an attempt to clear my name, I tracked down the source and made my case to the rumor- monger who admitted to not knowing the whole story, or at least my side of it. It was a wasted conversation because the word was already out and there was no taking it back. I thought it was ridiculous she supported her boss, the criminal, instead of me. It was more drama I didn't need in my life at the time.

I'd heard other rumors too about my personal life, one I later found to be true about my wife. The police service was like Peyton Place at times, where everyone talked about everyone else's business. Years earlier, I overheard two dispatchers talking about how my wife and I had separated. The funny part was the gossip didn't even know who I was, and I was sitting across the table from her.

When working with others, in close proximity for eight hours or more a day, it can be difficult not to get involved in each other's lives off the job. Some liked to whine and complain about their other halves, but I never said anything to anyone except my best friend. I was there to do a job, and not to share my personal life with anyone who'd listen.

I enjoyed my job, most of the time. It wasn't always fun, or easy, but it was satisfying to me, and gave me a sense of accomplishment and self-worth. Sometimes I liked to think outside the box and throw out new ideas, but I always got the job done.

I did what they paid me to do and then some. There were very few detectives who instigated their own investigations from informant information, as I did. The majority of cops I knew took reactive policing in stride, following up and chasing leads after the crime. An old warhorse once told me not to re-invent the wheel. But it was always in my nature to look for a better way to make it turn.

The city didn't stand still because one of its finest was out of commission. I noticed his crew thrown out-of-whack, and slacking off. That left more for my people to do. But I knew we could handle it and we did. There was some talent on the other shift, but they seemed to be more followers, than the doers and future leaders I had under my wing.

Twenty-Eight

Broken

Chen sat on the edge of the bed and tested her legs. Still a bit wobbly, she got up, walked to the window, and pulled the curtains back. The only view was the brick wall on the building next door. She could tell it was daylight, but nothing else. Turning around to check out the room, she found it was nothing like her former luxury accommodations.

The only furniture in the room was the wooden bed, a nightstand, and a mismatched dresser with an old mirror mounted on the wall above it. The floor was carpeted but heavily soiled and had probably never been cleaned. The duffle bag that contained everything Chen owned was at the foot of the bed. She stared at the door, walked over to it, and reached for the handle.

The door swung in, crunching her fingers and bumping her head. She stumbled back as a young Asian man stepped into her room. He said it was good she was awake, since he couldn't properly welcome her to her new home while she was sleeping. The man removed the belt from his pants and held it in one hand.

He told her to take off her clothes, and lie on the bed. Naked, Chen teared up and began to quiver when she climbed onto the bed. The man dropped his pants and laid down beside her. He said there would be no rich sugar daddy to pamper her, and she was going to learn how to properly please a man.

He grabbed the back of her head and forced her face into his crotch, his hot and hard flesh pressed up against her cheek. She'd never seen a man's thing up close before, the room was always dark when Mr. Wong visited. The man kept a grip on her ponytail and told her how to use her mouth to please him. Chen began to cry.

He showed no mercy and told her she could blubber all she wanted, and to put his cock in her mouth. The man moved her head up and down and told Chen what to do until she gagged on the appendage being forced down her throat. He complained about her teeth and small mouth, then pushed her back on the bed and got on top of her. Even though she knew from experience what came next, Chen tensed up. It only made things worse as the man forced himself inside her.

The rest of the encounter was a blur and Chen wondered if she'd passed out at one point. The man wasn't as gentle as Mr. Wong, and he took longer to use her. She laid there sobbing after he left her room. She thought about the Wong's and their penthouse, maybe it wasn't so bad after all. Her thoughts drifted to home and she wondered how her family was.

Her bedroom door opened and another Asian man came in. He smiled, took off his clothes, and took his turn with her. This time she really did pass out. She wasn't sure, but thought yet a different man was on top of her when she regained consciousness.

Chen's mind went blank. She thought she'd died, and gone to hell.

Twenty-Nine

Sneak & Peek

I was sweating my ass off on the EFX machine when Tina Farmer caught up with me in the gym.

"Hey Storm, sorry to bug you during your workout...I'm putting my information together for the general warrant. I've confirmed Warren Willis lives there; the house is in his mother's name but he pays the utilities. Electric bill isn't abnormally high but he probably doesn't need the extra lighting with the greenhouse...could have bypassed the service box...you've seen it before."

I grabbed my sweat towel and wiped my face. Farmer was new to the drug squad but a fast learner, and she seemed to take full advantage of the informant I gave to her. Sometimes investigators made great cases by acting on information supplied by their CIs. It had worked out well for me.

Tina looked on while I caught my breath. She was an attractive woman and a decent street cop. Her only mistake so far in her career was hooking up with a married male cop. He eventually left his wife for her, but then broke Tina's heart and moved on. I found her easy to look at, but felt she was high-maintenance emotionally and not my type.

Honestly, in considering her previous beau, I knew I wasn't pretty enough to catch her eye.

"Anyway, I need to source your informant info for the warrants...I'm preparing the drug warrant too so we're ready to go if we get a good look in the greenhouse. Has your CI proven reliable in the past?"

It was a good question, and she needed an answer to satisfy the Justice reading her warrant application. A single reliable source might be enough to obtain the sneak and peek warrant, but two independent sources were normally required for a drug search warrant. A man's home is his castle and all that. I considered who Lisa was to me, and how I believed her. I fudged.

"Yes, Tina, proven reliable once before...netting me some counterfeit money...but leave that part out, it might burn her with your target if his circle is small. You can say I've known the CI for six years (which was true) and she's supplied other information that was accurate but not acted upon in relation to a criminal prosecution."

She smiled. "Sounds good to me, I'll make it work. Enjoy your workout...I'll let you know how we make out."

Thirty

New Friends

It seemed like Chen slept for days. She was stiff and sore all over, and had to pee badly. The grogginess was completely gone, and she suddenly remembered her living nightmare. The bed felt damp. When she rolled over, she found blood and bodily fluid stains. Realizing she was naked; the abused young woman noted the area below her stomach and above her legs. She had to find a bathroom.

Walking to the door was a chore in itself, her legs were stiff, and the tender skin inside her thighs felt like it was on fire. She wrapped a bedsheet around herself. Finding the door unlocked, she peeked into the hall and saw at least four other rooms. Chen headed towards them and saw another girl through the open door of the first room.

She paid no particular attention to Chen but pointed further down the hall for the bathroom. Chen was in no mood to make friends or in any condition to stop and talk. She found the bathroom and locked herself in. It was nothing like the one in the Wong's penthouse, but there was a bathtub and the hot water worked.

Chen soaked in the tub and gingerly tended to the sore area between her legs. It was sensitive even to her touch. Her eyes welled up. She laid back and closed them tight, slowly sliding under the water. Holding her breath, Chen hoped it was all a bad dream and everything would be better when she surfaced and opened her eyes. It wasn't.

She gasped for air. There was a knock on the door, and a girl told her to hurry up, that they all had to share the bathroom. The voice disappeared but Chen pulled the plug anyway. She didn't need any other enemies in her new home.

She returned to her bedroom and dressed in fresh clothes. A young woman stood at the door. She was about the same age as Chen and introduced herself. Her name was Pepper and everyone had a nickname there. If she didn't pick one, they would do it for her. The girl said she got hers because she was so energetic. Chen understood and had a hard time keeping up. Pepper spoke rapidly in both English and Mandarin.

Her self-appointed new friend told her not to lock the bathroom or her bedroom door, that they didn't like that. She told her to practice English whenever she could, and she would earn better tips that way. Pepper said she hoped Chen got lots of rest because she and the other girls had been very busy lately. She went on about how poor she was when she got there, but the money she saved would enable her to travel to America where she would become rich and famous.

No wonder they call her Pepper, Chen thought. She asked about the other girls and her new friend said Chen made four. They each had their own bedroom, where they slept and entertained gentlemen callers. She said there was a kitchen and living room downstairs, and if she wanted,

Chen could meet the other girls. Pepper asked if she was hungry, and said to follow her to where they kept food in the fridge. She said they had to do their own cooking but she didn't know how, and that if she was nice to Sunshine, she might cook for her.

Chen asked why they called her Sunshine. Pepper said it was because she never smiled and had a very dark complexion. She might have African in her blood. The girl cooked for Pepper and made good rice and scrambled eggs. Pepper asked Chen if she liked eggs. She said someone drops them off and because they keep their own chickens, the girls don't have to pay for them.

Chen was still stiff and sore, and listening to Pepper gave her a headache. She thought she might feel better if she ate something. A young Asian man she hadn't seen before sat in a recliner in the living room playing video games on the television. He didn't bother to look up when the girls entered the room.

She asked Pepper where the other girls were and she said they were still in bed. They had late night visitors. The energizer bunny said she never slept in and mornings were the best part of the day. She added Fawn was supposed to come by and take them shopping for clothes so they could look nice for clients.

Before Chen could ask, Pepper said that Fawn was the woman who checked up on them and took them to the doctor. She was older and Shooter said she used to service clients just like them. The chatterbox assumed she was promoted. Fawn had nice clothes and jewelry and drove a fancy car. She was supposed to be there by noon. Pepper said they better wake the other girls.

Chen asked if it was Shooter who was playing the video game and yappy wondered how she knew. It was an educated guess since he'd been killing zombies the whole time. Chen opened and looked into the fridge. She spotted some yogurt, and asked if she could have some. Pepper told her to take what she wanted but to mark it on the list so Fawn knew what needed replacing.

She rambled on about how Jasmine never marked anything down because she was a lazy bitch, and how she herself, had to keep an accurate count of everything. She added that Fawn told her she was OCD, whatever that meant, and that it sounded like a disease or something.

The kitchen door swung open and a worn but attractive Asian woman walked in. She sniffed the air and looked around, not paying any particular attention to the younger girls. She asked where the other two were. They were supposed to be ready, and she had no time to wait on the little whores.

Pepper said they were still sleeping, and she was about to wake them. They had late night guests. Fawn cut her off, saying she didn't care and it wasn't her problem. The older woman said the place smelled of sweaty men and stale pussy, and she'd be outside in the car. On her way out, she said the bus was leaving in five minutes, with or without them.

Thirty-One

Stumped

I bumped into Blackjack in the hallway that connected our two offices. He paused and told me his gang took down a huge forced grow operation at Warren Willis' house the previous afternoon. Before picking up his pace again, my buddy told me to come and see him when I had a minute. There was something seized during the raid I should see.

It was a busy morning and I didn't get to the Drug Squad office until around eleven. Blackjack was preparing samples of the drugs they seized, to send away for analysis. I made myself comfortable in the empty chair in front of his desk. Without looking up, he handed me several pages of photocopied money they found during the Willis raid.

He gave me a minute. "See anything unusual?"

I flipped through pages of Canadian currency. Photocopies were used to prove the seizure and put into the charge files prepared for court.

"Yeah, they're all hundred-dollar bills...no small stuff...unusual to say the least."

"Anything else?"

I kept turning pages and then I saw it. "Holy shit...some of the serial numbers are the same."

"Yep, I counted five different ones. The money is counterfeit...didn't you tell me bills like those were turning up around town?"

"I did...how much is here?"

"Twenty thousand...in two bundles, a hundred bills in each."

"Willis could be our printer...any other evidence seized, like paper or copiers?"

Blackjack sat back in his chair and rolled his eyes. "Nothing in the reports...I called the Stump and woke him up. His statement says he found the cash in a desk drawer in the office."

Stump was the nickname I'd given the man because he was as dumb as one, and he probably should have stayed in traffic enforcement.

Blackjack continued. "He said a photocopier, paper, and other office supplies were in the room, but he assumed it had something to do with whatever work Willis did. The focus of their search was mainly the greenhouse so they didn't tear the house apart."

I glanced up at the clock behind Blackjack. "Fuck! Has Willis been released yet?"

"I know what you're thinking...I'm way ahead of you. I already called the cellblock and they think Willis might make bail...and yes, I told them to make sure the money is real. At my request, dispatch sent a patrol car to sit on his place. The warrant expired at midnight last night but I gave instructions not to let anyone in. Hopefully I don't get burned by someone else who has a right to be in there."

Blackjack nodded along while I suggested we needed another warrant to get back in the house. He had an uncanny knack of knowing what I was thinking, or was about to say.

"I called Farmer too and told her to get her ass back in here. If you and someone from Fraud can give her a few paragraphs on the counterfeit angle, she can do a C.C. warrant focusing on the manufacturing equipment Stump saw in plain sight, in the same location as the bogus bills. That should be enough to get it signed. Can your CI give you anything more?"

"No, she only knew about the weed. She passed off some of the C-notes but didn't know where they came from. Need anything else from me?"

"Not really, but someone from Fraud should probably go along. You can too, if you want."

I got up to leave his office. "Yeah, I'll tag along...have Farmer drop me a dime once the warrant is signed. How'd they make out with the grow-op?"

"A hundred and fifty plants...half of them harvested. Good thing we hit the place when we did. He had twenty pounds of weed packaged and ready to go."

Blackjack's phone rang and I headed back to my office.

Thirty-Two

Money Maker

We executed another search warrant at Warren Willis' residence and discovered a counterfeit money operation that would later make him famous.

The following are actual excerpts from 'WIKIPEDIA':

Warren Willis (name changed) is one of Canada's most prominent counterfeiters. He succeeded in counterfeiting the Canadian hundred-dollar bill. They were the highest quality computer produced counterfeits of Canadian currency to date. Between ten and nineteen percent of retailers nation-wide refused accepting 100-dollar bills as payment, due to the difficulty of identifying the fake copies.

Willis grew up in the Windsor area and considered himself a computer nerd in high school. By the age of 13 he was able to produce his first fake bills. After high school, Willis studied bioscience and mechanical engineering in university. By the age of 26 he had purchased a condominium, Ferrari, and various other luxury vehicles.

During his teenage years Willis was able to forge all kinds of documents, including insurance certificates, welfare cards, checks and gift certificates. He did jail time for forgery. After that he spent weeks tinkering with scanned copies of bank notes to perfect the simulated images and security features using techniques he found on websites. He used editing software and printed more than 7.7 million dollars using an HP Deskjet printer.

He used special paper as well as custom foil to forge the metallic patch on the bills. Willis also used fluorescent paint to simulate the green dots. A police raid netted over a quarter of a million dollars in fake bills. About a year later, after the dust had settled and Willis was in jail, over 40,000 bills had been detected and taken out of circulation. His fame led the History Channel to film a documentary about his escapades.

The raid made many people happy, and not just police services across the country. Merchants and financial institutions offered a collective sigh of relief. Our Chief was ecstatic about the bust, and called a press conference to let the Fraud Squad do a show and tell in front of the news media. The huge weed bust from the previous day wasn't mentioned.

News travels fast. My CI, Joey, called to see if he could get in on any reward action for the information he provided. After the media storm, someone from the Toronto Police finally got back to me about Lisa's fraud charges. After I laid out how her tip led us to the counterfeiter, he assured me he would talk to their Crown Attorney and get back to me.

Our Fraud Squad was more than happy, being able to close a bunch of their cases. They even managed to collect overtime hours, something that never happened with their steady day job. With all the reports completed, two of them joined me, and the Drug Squad for beer and wings. We all had a good laugh when one of the Fraud guys produced a hundred-dollar bill and offered to buy a round.

Thirty-Three

Growing Up

Chen lay on her bed, staring out the window at the wall next door. She counted the bricks one by one, recalling each year of her life, trying to remember what it was like to be a child. Technically, she was a teenager, but in actuality she'd become a woman. *What is it like to be a teenager?* She wondered.

If she lived back home, she'd be in high school and meeting new friends. The only so-called friends she had now were other girls like her, all kidnapped, or sold into the sex trade. Chen had no idea how it all worked. She slowly added pieces to the puzzle, and it started to form a picture. She knew her father owed money to someone, and that was why they took her from her family.

She knew there was some type of network in place that moved them around and turned them all into prostitutes. Chen wondered how Mr. Wong was involved. She didn't think about it at first, but after listening in on some of his phone conversations, and the way he got rid of her, she couldn't help but think some of his business dealings had to do with women like her.

Whether Chen liked it or not, she soon fell into the routine of living and working in a bawdy house. Being the new girl proved to be good and bad. Many of the regular clients asked for her and she started to receive tips from them. On the flipside, it made the other girls jealous, causing them to complain, and lash out at her.

Every new day was a learning experience for Chen Shen, but with each one, she became more distraught, lonelier, and homesick. Pepper was always the optimist, trying to cheer her up by planting false visions in Chen's head, like her own dream of being a famous celebrity in America someday.

Chen got along with the other girls the best she could, but suspected one of the other two was sneaking into her room searching for money. Thankfully, she discovered a loose floorboard concealed by one of her bed legs. Building her bankroll was harder than she thought. Chen learned they paid for what she thought were free groceries. Fawn, the woman who took them shopping, was quite clear when she told them nothing was free, and like in any other household, they had to pay their fair share.

Chen wondered if the two young men who took shifts watching the house had to pay for what they ate and drank. They were always in the fridge helping themselves to stuff the girls bought. Chen didn't even know their names. Pepper told her they couldn't associate with the girls, and if they tried any funny business, they would be *disappeared*. She said it happened when she first got there, and one of them got friendly with her. Not knowing any better, she had sex with the man. Somebody ratted him out and he was gone the next day.

Thinking about food, Chen decided she was hungry, and went downstairs to see what she could scrounge. Her babysitter stared to the TV screen, and his thumbs banged away at the game buttons as usual. She called the guy's Shooter and Tooter, the latter because he constantly stunk up the room with rancid farts.

After making herself a sandwich, and grabbing a bottle of water, Chen walked over to the front door to look outside. Shooter looked up and stared at her. The door and anywhere outside of it, was off limits. She sighed and returned to her room.

Thirty-Four

Arora Borealis

It was somewhere around midnight, by the time I hit the road and started my long ride home. I probably had a dozen rye and diet cokes in me, but ate twice during the evening. That was my buzz management plan, eating enough to soak up the alcohol. It seemed to work for me and I was told by more than one person, I held my booze well, and didn't show the usual symptoms of consumption.

I probably shouldn't have been driving. It had been a long day and I was beat, but not one to get drowsy behind the wheel at night. If anything, I got head-bobs on the way home after working the day shift. With no traffic late at night, the drive home was relaxing and peaceful.

I was about half-way there, somewhere between the towns of McGregor and Harrow, when streams of light in the sky caught my eye. They lit up the blackness above the horizon, coming from the direction of Windsor. Blinking hard to take a better look, I noticed the illumination moved like waves of water in an off shore breeze. Curious, I pulled over and stopped on the shoulder.

A nip in the air tickled my ear when I rolled down the window. It looked like strobe lights in slow motion, dancing across the northern sky. I'd only caught a glimpse of something like that twice in my lifetime. It was the Northern Lights; a phenomenon rarely visible because of our southern locale, and the interference of artificial city lights. It was something to see. I felt like a kid staring at the moon wondering if it was made of cheese. Witnessing such things made me feel small and insignificant in universal terms.

Stars and the infinity of space always drew my curiosity, and I loved debating the possibility of extraterrestrial life. I could have sat there and stared into the sky all night but headlights appeared in my rearview mirror and I thought it best to move on. With my mind focused on my place in the world, I couldn't help but think about my marital situation. I tried so hard to get answers from Sandra, but they never seemed to be the ones I wanted to hear.

Knowing the sound of my vehicle's engine from a block away, the dog was waiting for me when I walked in the door. It was late and the house was quiet, I presumed my wife was upstairs sleeping. Brandy gave a little 'woof', her way of saying she wanted out to pee. I let her out the patio door and stepped out onto the deck while she went about her business.

I couldn't see the Arora Borealis from my house because of the tall trees north of me. The water in my pond resembled black ink and reflected the spattering of stars in the sky above me. My neighborhood was completely quiet. Even the frogs and fish were sleeping. Brandy spoke to me again, suggesting we call it a night, so off to bed we went.

Lying in bed, I thought about Sandra in the next bedroom. The arrangements had nothing to do with the crap we were going through. It was something we'd come up with years earlier to deal with my crazy shiftwork and her disrupted sleep. With the current situation, it felt like we were separated and living in the same house.

When my alarm went off in the morning it felt like I hadn't slept at all. Knowing we had a full crew in that day, and I earned Brownie points the day before, I called my boss and left him a message saying I'd be taking a lunch hour at the start of my shift. It wasn't an unusual request and something we did on occasion. I reset my alarm, rolled over and went back to sleep.

Thirty-Five

On the Move Again

Early one morning, Chen awoke to the sound of her door hitting the wall. Her eyes popped open, and she found Fawn standing over her bed shouting at her to hurry and pack. They were all going on a trip. She knew better than to ask where, but did anyway. Fawn laughed and said they got their wish. They were going to America. Chen said America was Pepper's wish, not hers.

The older woman said they'd like it and would make lots of money there. She laughed when Chen complained she didn't have a passport, and said they took care of that, and she could pay them back later. Chen fussed again, asking why she should pay to go somewhere she didn't want to go. Fawn snapped back and demanded she pack.

Still groggy from sleep, but with little to pack, Chen was almost ready when Shooter and Tooter entered her room. They began to search by pulling out her drawers and checking under the mattress. Happy she had removed her stash from the floor only seconds before the men came in, Chen stepped into the hallway.

Fawn grabbed her duffle bag and dumped the contents onto the floor. After searching through Chen's belongings, she pointed to the bathroom, told her to go inside and take off her clothes. Chen wasn't happy, but had no choice in the matter. She went in and got undressed, removing her panties quickly and bunching them into a ball in one hand.

Fawn stared like a hawk eyeing its next meal. She demanded Chen's money, saying it would be used for the trip. Chen played dumb and shrugged as if she didn't understand. Fawn's eyes locked onto her hand holding the underwear. The retired whore said to give her the money or she would forcefully take it.

One of the other girls told her it wasn't a good idea to challenge or mess with Fawn. Chen dropped her gaze to the floor and held out her clinched hand. The wicked matron removed the cash and threw the panties in her face. She told her to get dressed and repack her bag. It was time to go.

Downstairs, Chen found the other girls packed and waiting. They appeared as miserable as she did, with the exception of Pepper. She wore a toothy smile that stretched from ear to ear, and asked Chen if she was excited about going to America, where she would become a movie star.

She stared at the clueless girl in disbelief. Did Pepper really think that would ever happen? Maybe it was her wishful thinking that kept herself going. Chen remembered when she hoped she would be rescued and able to return home. She grew more convinced every day it was never going to happen. America was even further from home. A burning sensation in her gut told her she would never see her family again.

Thirty-Six

Training

In all honesty, police work is not that exciting. I can't remember if I read it somewhere or heard it explained in a movie. About ninety-nine percent of the time, the job is boring and non-eventful. The other one percent is like running around with your hair on fire. Our annual in-service training fell into the larger percentile.

Every time there's a high-profile incident where the police are involved, and it doesn't conclude with a fairytale ending, armchair quarterbacks publicly denounce the officers involved and call for more and better training so they can learn to be perfect at everything they do. Those same critics have no idea of the hundreds of training hours police officers go through every year of their career.

For veteran cops like myself, in-service training was nothing but a pain-in-the-ass. We did our best to make excuses to get out of the course, or at least to skip a few classes. The brass was well aware of that fact. While in training themselves, they took to taking daily attendance and did their best to keep us awake during those boring lectures or films...especially when the lights were out.

Some of the topics were actually interesting, like show and tell when they put all sorts of seized weapons on display and we played with them. It was subjects like first aid and CPR, I hated. What the young ambitious teachers didn't understand was how methods of treatment had changed over my twenty-four years on the job. The number of breaths and chest compressions varied from year to year. How did they expect us to remember it all?

Self-defense training was the same. Chokeholds and other containment techniques I learned as a recruit, either changed or became illegal. I lost track of how many ways, over the years, they showed me how to subdue and hand-cuff someone. It was part of the job; learning new laws, and keeping up with changes...our uniforms and the assortment of weapons we carried included.

When I became a Constable, I was issued a twelve-inch nightstick, a pair of handcuffs, and a .38 caliber revolver. Years later we changed to a shorter barreled .38 and instead of carrying six loose bullets in a pouch, they gave us two six-round speed-loaders. When I joined the Drug Squad, we were the first to transition to the .40 caliber semi-automatic pistol. It came with two ten-round magazines, and more lethal ammunition.

Because certain folks thought police were shooting and killing people for no good reason, they issued us pepper spray and asps (expandable steel batons). The experts came up with what they called a 'use of force' chart. This colorful wheel laid out which soft or hard contact weapons police should use in different situations. I called it the Wheel of Fortune.

Then, as if uniformed police officers didn't have enough shit to carry, the public thought cops should have Tasers to avoid the use of deadly force. In that split second where a police officer has to make a decision on how to save their life or someone else's, they have to spin the wheel of fortune and choose the right weapon for the situation. I believe in something else I once heard: It's better to tried by twelve, than carried by six.

In-service training normally ran for a week and I had a court appearance on the Wednesday. It gave me a chance to break up the monotony, and miss pumping the chest of a rubber dummy or getting tased to see what it felt like. It was the same with pepper spray...they said we needed to know what it felt like. Thankfully, we didn't have to shoot each other to see how it felt.

Thirty-Seven

Going to America

The girls were in the van and on the road all day and into the night, sleeping and eating junk food. As usual, any view outside the vehicle was purposely blocked. Chen awoke to the sound of slamming doors and male voices. The driver had stopped, and judging by the lack of street noise, she assumed he drove into some kind of garage or warehouse.

She was right. Ordered out of the van, they were directed toward a larger transport truck. There was nothing in the dimly lit building but the vehicles and Asian men Chen didn't know. One of them opened the back of the truck and snapped his head sideways, motioning for them to get inside.

Groggy, and with wobbly legs from sleep and lack of motion, she shuffled to the new conveyance. A half dozen more young Asian women were already in the truck. Chen got a sinking feeling in her stomach, where were they really going and what would happen to them now? She glanced at Fawn for a clue but the woman was already getting back into her van.

More road travel in darkness, Chen heard a few whimpers and then whispers from the girls around her. A few exchanged names and others tried to guess where they were going. In her usual exultant fashion, Pepper announced they were on their way to America where they would all make lots of money and she would become a movie star. Chen knew better.

With all she'd been through since her kidnapping, there was no reason to think anything would be different where ever they were going. Once an innocent young girl with dreams of maybe becoming a ballerina someday, she was now nothing more than a sex slave. If they really were going to America, why would it be any different?

Chen used her duffle bag as a pillow and stretched out across the dirty wood floor. She bumped one of the other girls and was kicked for invading her space. Chen tried to clear her mind and sleep. It was becoming impossible to ignore the stench of their waste pail and sound of another girl vomiting. Someone mentioned the girl might be pregnant and feared what would happen to her when her condition was discovered.

Brief moments of relief came when the truck stopped for gas. The poop pail was dumped and they received food and water. Chen filled her lungs with as much fresh air as she could when the door was open. Since her captors never exposed their cargo when other people were around, the view outside offered no clues as to where they were.

The monotonous days and nights on the road ended with another warehouse transfer. This time the accommodations looked all too familiar. It was another shipping container and another group of young women. Chen scanned the new faces and noted the same looks of despair that she'd been experiencing since leaving home.

The heat, cold, and unsanitary conditions became part of her daily life. Chen tried to be optimistic and thought where ever she ended up, it had to be better than the hell she was in now. She read and heard stories about America, how people lived free there. What, exactly, would that mean for someone like her?

Her time in the shipping container seemed longer. When the door opened and a blast of cold air took her breath away, Chen knew she was no longer in Asia. The chill sunk into her skin but it was invigorating. Strangely, somewhere deep inside her heart, she felt a glimmer of hope. Perhaps America would offer her salvation and even freedom someday. It was doubtful in her current situation. Hope was key to her survival.

Thirty-Eight

Confidential Informants

After a week of brushing up on the law and all the non-lethal ways of busting bad guys without killing them, I used my Saturday off to do a landscaping job for my sister. Gaining credibility with exploits in my own back yard, the oldest of my three female siblings offered to pay me for my time and expertise.

She wanted a small water feature installed in her back garden. Although a millionaire, her husband was too cheap to pay a professional landscape company and expected a family discount. The job took most of the day. After a few beers to admire my work, they invited me to stay for dinner.

My CI, Joey interrupted my meal. A traffic cop stopped him for speeding. He called me immediately, and arrogantly handed his phone to the officer. His selfish act put both the cop and me in an awkward position, but we both had enough experience to deal with the situation. Without getting into too much detail, I explained who Joey was to me and our police service. I told the officer to use his own discretion as to whether or not he issued a ticket.

As it turned out, the traffic cop thought he owed me because of a drug raid I conducted at a house next door to his parents. The dealers were a scourge to the neighborhood, and my action resulted in them moving. I thanked the officer and he put Joey back on the line. I did my best at delivering a lecture, but knew my words went in one ear and out the other. Joey laughed and said he owed me one. He had a few grams of cocaine in the car.

Questioned by my sister who'd overheard the conversation, I tried to explain how things worked in my world, while I finished dinner. I knew her hubby understood, he simply smiled and went outside for a smoke. The quizzical look never left her face; she couldn't quite comprehend how things really worked behind the scenes.

When I got home that night, the dog, my wife, and all her personal belongings were gone. I wasn't surprised. We talked about letting the dog stay with her parents since neither of us spent much time at home anymore. She'd also mentioned looking for her own place, but I didn't expect it to happen so quickly. Something fuzzy brushed my leg while I stood in the kitchen. Why the hell didn't she take her cat?

Food always made me feel better. I ignored the low-carb regimen I'd been on and made myself a box a Kraft Dinner with extra cheese. It was too chilly for sitting outside so I perched in my chair at the dining room table. The spot offered a view of the pond. The season had brought hibernation and death to my garden. I couldn't help but feel sorry for myself.

My mobile phone rang. I raced to shove the last few bites of pasta in my mouth before I even considered answering. The call display showed a Detroit number so I let it go to voicemail, while I considered where my life was headed. I waited for the message light to come on and checked the recording. It was a Detroit homicide detective, inquiring about one of my drug informants who'd been killed.

Ronald Davis lived in the west side projects in Windsor and had family on the other side of the border. He supplied me with information on at least a half dozen crack dealers, his motivation being his own habit and the need for cash. It had been almost a year since I'd heard from him and was curious about what happened, but I was in no mood to return the call.

Deciding to get some fresh air and clear my head, I threw on a coat and went for a walk down the street, to the lake. Sitting on the park bench I stared at the grey sky and even greyer water, I contemplated life. In my opinion, it had been a good run to that point. If only I understood where things went wrong.

Thirty-Nine

Welcome to Canada

The next breath of fresh air Chen took was in a place she overheard one of her captor's call, Montreal. She heard of the city in school, a place early European explorers discovered when they entered the North American continent from the Atlantic Ocean. Montreal was located in Canada. She was sure of it.

They took the girls to a huge old house in the intercity. Once inside, they were split into groups of four per room. Dirty old mattresses were laid out for them. Chen was puzzled. There were only two mattresses and four young women in her room.

Her question was answered by as skinny orange-haired Asian woman who introduced herself simply, as Mother. She said they would be sharing the mattresses, and it wouldn't be a problem because two of them would be working while the other two slept. Before anyone could question her, Mother raised a hand for silence and ordered everyone to be downstairs in ten minutes.

They gathered in the living room, and the woman, who looked like the Asian version of Raggedy Ann, with a makeup job that resembled something you might see on a clown, laid out the house rules. She told the women they would be learning to dance. Chen felt a spark of excitement at the possibility of fulfilling her dream but there was no flame.

They were to become exotic dancers and work in a nearby strip club. Mother emphasized the words 'strip club', which caused whispers and muttering among the group. One young woman spoke up and said she didn't know how to dance.

The older woman said that was of no concern, that they simply take off their clothes and wiggle their body to the music. The horny men watching wouldn't care if they knew how to dance or not. She went on to explain they had to follow the club manager's rules, without exception, and do whatever was required. They would work in shifts and be confined to the house when they were not dancing at the club. Mother wanted to know if there were any questions but no one had the nerve to ask.

Back in her room, Chen and her fellow inmates eyed their sleeping arrangements and started to debate how to share the accommodations. Once again, Mother showed up in their doorway and pointed at two of the women. They were to dance first, and be ready in ten minutes. Confused and sorrowful expressions donned all their faces after Mother left. The two selected girls left and Chen was happy she didn't have to go first.

Her new roommate introduced herself as Ling, and asked where Chen was originally from. The two of them relaxed on their mattresses, chatted, and wondered aloud what was in store for them. Both agreed they were glad the other two girls had to dance first. About an hour later, Mother entered their room with two men and told Chen and Ling to have sex with them.

Forty

No Rest for the Broken-Hearted

Standing in front of my desk, I looked at the mess of paperwork on top of it. I hoped it was all Shorty's stuff. Thankfully, most of it was. The hockey shit had nothing to do with police work. It was no surprise he didn't accomplish anything while I was off. I found an empty banker's box, shoveled his stuff into it, and threw it on top of a file cabinet behind my desk.

When I turned around my boss was standing there.

"You know he won't be able to reach it up there."

"That's the point. Looks like he was busy while I was away."

"His crew was...didn't see him around much, as usual. Whenever I ask what he's up to, he tells me how swamped he is."

I sat down and flipped through the post-it notes stuck to my incoming tray.

"Yeah, but it's hockey season, and the swamp's frozen."

Brian Gamble laughed.

"Hey, did you get a call from Detroit Homicide? Sounded pretty important—something about one of your informants and a murder investigation. One of those notes is from me, with the detective's number. Any idea what it's all about?"

"A dead rat, but I didn't answer the call or get back to him yet. Rough weekend...Sandra moved out."

He shook his head. "Sorry to hear that. Been there...if you need someone to talk to..."

Two of the Constables walked into the office and Gamble stopped talking. He reached out and patted me on the shoulder, and headed back to his office.

I flipped through the notes and found the one with the Detroit detective's number on it. Looking at the message light flashing on my phone, I decided to check for a voice message from him first, so he'd at least get the impression I paid attention to his calls. My mailbox was full and his message only said he'd try my cell phone.

The homicide dick answered on the second ring, and said he was just catching up on paperwork. He told me they found one of my old business cards from the Drug Squad, hidden in Ronald Davis's wallet, and wanted to know my involvement with him. I explained he was a drug informant in the Windsor crack subculture, and that I hadn't seen him in about a year.

The detective asked if I had any knowledge of Davis dealing crack cocaine in Windsor or Detroit. I told him I only knew him as an addict and heavy user. The Detroit investigator explained my old CI was shot and killed, during what looked like a drug deal gone bad. He added they identified a second victim as Davis's cousin. He asked if he had any other family on my side of the border.

I told the American cop I'd dig up what we had and email or fax it to his office. He gave me his contact information and thanked me for my help. I had completely forgotten about Ronny. Some informants stayed in touch and others just disappear.

Another of my phone messages was from the Toronto cop I connected with about Lisa's criminal case. It was a courtesy call to say he passed on the information about the counterfeit bust to the Assistant Crown Attorney handling her case. The cop said he couldn't make any promises but the ACA sounded impressed, and considering she had no previous record, said he'd ask for a conditional discharge. That was good news for my brother, who would have probably had to cover legal expenses when his stepdaughter went through the court process. I made a mental note to call him later on to share the news.

Listening to the remainder of my phone messages, I started a list of things to do the rest of the day and into the week.

About to get into my email, I realized we had a prisoner in custody and I had to get someone on the file. There seemed to be an extraordinary number of commercial break-ins over the weekend. My work was cut out for me. I called out to the Auto Squad that I could really use a bagel and a pop, and would buy if they were going to Timmies.

It seemed like only ten minutes, but the clock showed an hour later when Roxanne called. She heard the news about the counterfeit bust, and wondered if the owner of her club was implicated in any way. Not having the time to get into it with her, I said I'd have to get back to her later. She started to ask another question. I knew she was sniffing around for a reward. I cut her off and politely hung up.

Forty-One

Private Dancers

Chen had never been to Disney World, but she thought the strip club was like a big amusement park for horny men. The whole scene was a completely new experience for her. She had never seen so many round-eyes. It was like walking into a new school for the first time, she had no friends, and no idea of the curriculum.

Mother accompanied her to the club and pointed her to a closet full of skimpy and sweat-stained costumes. Chen held her breath as she sorted through worn and torn outfits, the scents of cheap perfume and body odor caught in the back of her throat. She felt her face flush as she imagined having to wear such clothes on stage in front of a room full of men.

She didn't dance that first night. Mother and the club manager threw so many rules at her she feared what would happen if she forgot even one. They told her to mingle, be seen, and watch how the other women performed on and off stage. If a man requested conversation or a lap dance, she was to comply.

When Chen stepped from the safety of the changing room into the main lounge, the loud music thumped in her chest. She fiddled with the near-empty bikini top; too large for her small breasts. The air smelled of booze and sweat and felt cool on her exposed skin. Nobody seemed to notice her as she slinked along the bar, making her way deeper into the room.

All eyes were on the woman on stage, who hung upside down on a brass pole with her private parts on display for everyone to see. Chen's jaw went slack at the sight. A man wearing a nice suit glanced in her direction and said something but she couldn't hear him over the music. When she bent down closer, he grabbed her by the ass and asked when she would be on stage. Instinctively, Chen scurried away.

Heading back towards the bar, she ran into a black man the size of an adult bear. Chen's gaze was on level with his belt buckle. He palmed the top of her head like a basketball and steered her into a room sectioned off by dark curtains. It was a bit quieter in there and the man crouched down to bring himself closer to her eye level. He introduced himself as Mike, the bouncer and doorman.

Chen had no idea what a bouncer was, but Mike spoke to her in a tone more polite than anything she experienced since she left home. He said she was supposed to be nice to the clients. It was his job to see they didn't go too far. Men weren't supposed to grope her whenever they pleased, but he couldn't watch them all at once. If he felt they were out of line, he would remove them from the club.

Mike took a few extra minutes of his time and showed her around the VIP room they were in, and explained what was legally allowed to happen in there. He said some men asked for more and if the women complied, the club could get in trouble with the cops. The big man winced and looked around as if he was checking to see who was watching. He went on to say he knew some of the girls were having sex with clients, but he preferred it take place elsewhere.

Chen liked the bouncer. He was the largest man she ever saw; even bigger than the one who kidnapped her from her home. She followed Mike out of the VIP room, trying to stay in his shadow. When he got to the front door, she found herself standing alone. Chen felt like a flightless little bird in a room full of hungry wolves.

Forty-Two

Smoke 'em if You Got 'em

I skimmed through the commercial break-ins from the weekend, looking for patterns or similarities. Brazen thieves went on a crime spree, hitting three variety stores, and taking a ton of cigarettes and lottery tickets. Given the going price for a carton of smokes, the culprits were about to make some good money.

Noticing all the stores were in the west end of the city, my old informant Baby Street Bob came to mind. He was an old west-side rounder who knew everything that went on in his neighborhood. I busted Bob for selling crack and turned him into one of my best drug informants. He said he only sold the crack to buy weed, for medicinal purposes.

Baby Street Bob was hard-core, and the last guy you'd ever think was a rat. He looked like a mobster who had his nose busted more than once, and he had criminal convictions for assault and robbery. The last time he gave me information he was trying to keep a neighborhood drug dealer from selling to his grandson.

I assigned the store break-ins to one of my crew and gave old Bob a call. He was always careful when answering the phone at home and I was to ask for Richard whenever I called. It was his middle name, a clue to let him know it was me on the phone. It was like a secret handshake we never used because he always answered the phone.

My call took on a life of its own as I caught up with Bob. His grandson was off the dope, his wife had passed, and his arthritis was so bad he was smoking joints like they were cigarettes.

That was my cue to cut in.

"Sorry to hear all that...especially about your wife. I'm calling you about cigarettes...someone hit three stores in your neck-of-the-woods and stole a shit-load of smokes. I was wondering if you've heard anything or can point me in the right direction."

"Cheap smokes, eh? No, I haven't heard anything but I can put some feelers out and get back to you. Aren't you in Drugs anymore...why are you looking into B & E's?"

"Street Crimes now...they never keep us anywhere too long. Same shit, different dirt bags."

"Hey, I resemble that remark."

We both laughed and I told him to dime me if he heard anything. Bob agreed he would and hung up. I hadn't noticed while I was on the phone, Jim West had dropped off my bagel, Diet Pepsi, and my spare change. I sunk my teeth into the toasted multi-grain treat, while I read over the remainder of B & E reports.

It was after noon by the time I finished my morning paperwork. I looked at my list of things to do and said fuck it, I was going downstairs for a workout. With my gym bag in hand, passing West's desk on the way to the door, I heard a phone ring. He laughed.

"Sounds like yours, Norm."

"Yeah, what else is new?"

Thinking I'd still make my escape, I dropped the bag by the door and walked back to grab my phone. It was Bob.

"Wasn't sure if you still had the same mobile number and your call came up as private so I went through your switchboard. I've got something for you."

"That was quick...should I meet up with you somewhere?"

"No need since the old lady passed. We can talk on the phone. Dale Morneau's got your smokes, and a pile of lottery tickets."

Bingo! I figured Bob was right on since I didn't say anything about lottery tickets and busted Morneau before for drugs.

"I know him...think he did the B & E's?"

"No, he mostly fences shit these days...takes in stolen property for dope. He's in his mom's old place on Queen Street. My nephew scored me a carton of Players Navy Cut for forty bucks. You owe me fifty."

"What? Why do I owe you fifty?"

"My commission...any idea what a case of beer costs these days?"

"You old fucker, you'll never change. When did your nephew score the smokes?"

"Just before I called you. Says there are different brands and they were busy scratching a pile of lottery tickets looking for winners. Morneau was pissed off at how many losers there were. Hey, Norm, can't they track those through their computers?"

I remembered asking a store owner the same question when following up on a reported break-in and theft.

"From what I understand, only after they open the bundles and log them into the system, then they can tell where you bought the ticket...same for where it was stolen, I guess. Okay, I've gotta make some calls. You got my IOU for now and I'll get back to you later to let you know how we make out."

I hung up, looked across the room at my gym bag by the door, and sighed.

West had been listening in and chuckled. "No workout today, Storm. You got enough for a warrant?"

"Think so...gotta check next door with Drugs to see what else I can dig up on Dale Morneau...I thought he was still doing time for trafficking."

"Yeah...hurry up and do the time so you can get out and pull your next crime."

Forty-Three

New Job Worse than the Old Job

After giving up counting days on a calendar, Chen Shen couldn't remember how many weeks or even months she'd been working at the strip club in Montreal. They shuffled the women around between three different clubs and her life became a blur. When she wasn't dancing on stage or in men's laps, she was banging them in sleazy motel rooms.

The tips added up but in order to keep them she had to find creative ways to hide the money. Whenever she worked with Big Mike, he held her cash and kept an eye on her. The nicest man she'd ever met, he never asked her for anything. Unlike the other doormen, he even refused to take a portion of her tips.

The remaining bouncers, doormen, and managers were all ignorant perverts and no better than the horn dog customers that frequented the strip clubs. They all hinted around or came right out and told her they could take care of her if she took care of them. One doorman cornered her in a bathroom trying to get a blow job but the manager walked in on them. He fired the man on the spot but only because he kept her from making money working the floor.

Chen never liked or got used to having sex with strange men when she worked at the whorehouse in the old country. She learned to turn herself off and let them have their way with her, hoping it would all end quickly. Usually, it did. The Asian men couldn't seem to control themselves for very long. Unfortunately, that wasn't the case with the drunken men from the strip club.

She could never ignore what was happening to her body when she was pretending not to be there, but Chen learned to cope. It was the new job. She couldn't come to grips with being a stripper and prostitute. Having sex in a dark and dingy bedroom or hotel room was different from taking all her clothes off under bright lights, with every eye in the place roaming her naked body.

She felt it was demeaning. For some reason, disrobing and doing lap dances didn't seem as bad. Maybe it was the one-on-one experience, and the feeling she had more control of the situation. Being naked on stage in front of the whole world was something Chen didn't think she'd ever get used to. She wasn't alone in feeling that way. Some of the dancers used alcohol or drugs to cope.

She tried cocaine once and liked how it made her feel, but she didn't want to part with her hard-earned money to buy the stuff. Men in the clubs always bought her drinks, even though they were overcharged for the beverages. Most of the girls had an arrangement with bartenders to make them special non-alcoholic drinks. The clients were none the wiser and the dancers were able to make it through the night without becoming wasted.

Chen couldn't believe the money some men spent in the strip clubs. If they weren't handing over wads of cash, they were paying tabs with company credit cards. On a good night, she could make a few hundred dollars or more in tips. Her goal was to buy her way out of the whole nightmare someday.

Forty-Four

Proven Sources

With my guidance, Kristen Gelinas put together the information needed to obtain a search warrant for Morneau's residence on Queen Street. In order to satisfy a Justice, applicants have to justify their reasons for invading someone's privacy in the sanctity of their home. Police have to prove they believe is a criminal offence occurring there, giving them the grounds to conduct a search for evidence of that crime.

To do that, officers have to source all the information received. If it came from a confidential informant, police had to prove they were reliable in the past. Short of giving the CIs name and address, affiants have to reveal their relationship with the informant, including previous seizures or arrests where they assisted the police.

While I was filling her in about my CIs background, Kevin Bell stuck his head out of the boss's office and waved me in. Gelinas nodded she was fine and I should go ahead. Gamble and Bell were talking about the T & A strip club when I walked into the room.

Bell was the Sergeant in charge of the Morality Unit, and responsible for monitoring licensed liquor establishments throughout the city. I had worked with him for a short stint when I was in Morality, running a sting operation of the city's licensed escorts. We had also worked a few times together back in our uniformed patrol days.

There was an empty chair beside him, across from Gamble's desk, and I sat down. Bell turned to me once I'd settled.

"The boss tells me you've got someone inside T & A...an informant?"

"Yeah...one of the peelers...an old drug rat. I recently reconnected with her. She gave me info on bogus C-notes going around the club."

"Did she say anything about Asian dancers there?"

"Not much...only that there's a group of them there...something new to look at, I guess."

Staff Sergeant Gamble sat and listened. He took a different path up the ladder than Bell and I, and wasn't afraid to admit he wasn't as well versed in certain areas, where we had more experience and expertise.

"We've gotten a tip the Asian girls are being shipped down the 401 from the clubs in Montreal. Our *anonymous* source says he got the clap from one of the girls...apparently after hooking up in T & A. He took her to a local motel for sex and later discovered his dick was dripping. Test results said he had the clap and hepatitis."

"Dumb fuck...he didn't bag it?"

"Guess not...anyway...do you think your fink can get us the 411 on the Asian girls? We've been in there twice for drinks and lap dances, but they're pretty tight-lipped around strangers."

"You didn't use Shorty, did you?"

We all laughed out loud.

"No, not after he *blew it* at the massage parlor."

I laughed so hard my eyes watered. It's too bad Shorty wasn't around to defend himself. Using my fingers to pinch the top of my nose and regain my composure, I thought for a second before answering Bell's question.

"She's a junkie, but you'd never know it. She's a looker with intelligence, who knows the game, and doesn't mind making a little cash from us on the sly. I'll run it by her and keep you both in the loop."

Bell got up from his chair. "Thanks, Storm, you need any bodies for your search?"

"No, two of the Drug guys are coming along in case Morneau's got dope in the house...he sells coke and weed too. We should be good." I got up and turned for the door.

Gamble called out to me. "Looks like you might be working overtime...leave me a voicemail so I can brief the brass in the morning."

I glanced back. "Solve no crime before overtime."

Gelinas had put the finishing touches on her warrant by the time I got back to my desk. Knowing there was time to kill; I ordered a chicken-Caesar salad from an Italian restaurant down the street and slipped out to pick it up. After returning, and in between bites of my salad, I called next door and told the Drug guys to meet in my office for a briefing in a half hour.

Flipping through email on my computer, I remembered I needed to call Roxanne. Thinking about her last call to me, I wondered if she was pissed off when I hung up on her. There was no answer and my call went to voicemail. Kristen

Gelinas walked into the office wearing a smile. Her warrant was signed and ready to go.

Michael King had been out to the Queen Street address earlier, doing recon to find our best approach, and point of entry. He was finishing his map on the white board when the Drug guys came in. I gave Gelinas the nod and she used her partner's map to brief the entry team. It wasn't as if Morneau could flush cartons of cigarettes down the toilet, but we planned for a stealth approach and dynamic entry to surprise anyone in the home.

Everyone was busy double-checking their gear when Gamble wished us happy hunting. We filed out of the Street Crimes office and headed for our vehicles.

Forty-Five

Let's Dance

The few dance moves Chen picked up from watching the other girls on stage, seemed to be enough to draw attention from pervert's row—the drooling and horny men in the seats directly in front of the stage. She hated the probing stares that searched every inch of her body, but their approval meant tips, money thrown in her direction or stuffed into whatever skimpy outfit she might be wearing.

To Chen's delight, Big Mike started showing up at the other clubs to fill in when they were short-staffed. It gave her the chance to have a conversation with him one night, when it was quiet and she had some time to herself. The friendly giant said he sympathized with her. His mother, a prostitute, was killed by a john.

His grandmother raised him. She taught him to respect all women no matter who they were or what they did. Chen felt she could trust Mike and continued to give him her money to hold. She had run out of hiding places, and feared someone would steal her savings as they had in the past. Chen confided in her big friend. She hoped to escape one day and use the money to return home.

Mike told her the man who was in charge of the three clubs kept all the women's passports and ID locked in his vault. If he ever had the chance, he would try to get hers. Chen knew she wouldn't be able to flee the country without it, and the way it looked, she would be paying her father's debt for the rest of her life. In reality, she knew it was just an excuse to keep her as a sex slave.

On one occasion, when Chen gave Mike some of her tips, he asked if she wanted him to open a bank account for her. She wasn't sure, and never had one before. Chen asked him more about it. The big man said it was dangerous for him to keep cash around, and her stash was adding up to a nice sum. Mike told her the bank would keep her money safe and they would pay her to keep it there.

Chen wasn't quite sure what her friend meant but she thought it might be wise to take some of the other money she had hidden and put it in the bank. Mike assured her he would show her a bankbook so she would know he wasn't taking any of her money for himself. He said he made okay wages working at the strip clubs and some of the high rollers tipped him for getting them good seats.

The DJ called for Tinkerbell—the persona Chen chose as her stage name. Keeping her real name to herself was one of the only private things left in her life. Other than the owner, who was in possession of her ID, Big Mike was the only person in the club who knew her proper name. Her oversized bodyguard shrugged and tapped her shoulder with one of his bear paws. Chen rolled her eyes, offered Mike a flat smile, and headed for the stage.

Forty-Six

Lottery Loser

Surveillance on Morneau's house was still in place when we set up in a staging area around the block. An unknown male who'd gone into the house only minutes earlier was on his way out. I detailed two of my team to take him down once he got down the street. My purpose was to see if the man purchased and was in possession of stolen property.

If he was, it would confirm there were still stolen cigarettes in the house, and at the same time take some heat off my informant. After the raid, Morneau would no doubt wonder who ratted him out, and consider who bought stolen property from him before we showed up.

The man walked down Queen Street and met two plain clothed coppers when he turned the corner. He concealed two cartons of cigarettes under his coat and claimed he bought them at the corner store. The closest one was almost a half-mile away in the opposite direction. I had patrol officers hold him until we made our entry.

The front door was unlocked but as we entered, a large Pitbull charged the first man in. We came prepared and the second officer blasted the dog with a fire extinguisher. It never broke stride and ran right past us out the door and down the street. We found Morneau and another known criminal at the kitchen table scratching lottery tickets.

There was a pile of discarded losing tickets on the floor at their feet and fresh stacks of unchecked ones in front of them. The kitchen counter resembled a variety store shelf, with cartons of smokes all lined up and ready to sell. We arrested Morneau and his accomplice for possession of stolen property.

Michael King pointed to a small stack of scratch tickets in between the two men and asked, "How much did you win?"

Morneau replied, "Not even enough to pay for my fucking lawyer...these things are a rip off!"

We found a wad a cash in his pants pocket, and more in a kitchen drawer; just over two thousand in total. He wouldn't be able to use that for legal fees either, it was seized as proceeds of crime. From our count of the cigarettes still in the house, Morneau had sold quite a few. Over a hundred cartons remained, as well as a dozen stacks of unscratched lottery tickets. Several nickel bags of weed were found, along with a few grams of cocaine.

Both men were interviewed at HQ. Neither would admit to the store break-ins, of course, but Morneau commented he'd never pay for scratch tickets again because the majority of them were losers. He also asked if we knew what happened to his dog and wondered how we got by him at the front door.

After the raid, I drove into the housing projects where Baby Street Bob lived and dropped a dime. He met me in the parking lot around the corner a few minutes later. If I hadn't called him first, I might not have recognized him. The salt and pepper hair I remembered was now white, and his face and body looked hollow and thin. I didn't ask why, and assumed the hard-living life style was the reason for his sickly appearance.

Bob was happy to see me and offered his usual vice-grip handshake. He asked how the raid went and said it was fun working with me again. We chatted a bit but I cut it short, telling him I had a ton of paperwork to do, and I'd see to it he got a cash reward for helping me out.

Bob offered his hand again and said we had to get out for beers again some time. It was something he always brought up, referring to the first time we met at a local sportsmen's club. I said it sounded like a good idea and I'd give him a shout when his cash was available. Watching him shuffle toward home I wondered if it was true only the good die young.

Forty-Seven

No Money No Honey

Tinkerbell grew to be quite popular in the Montreal strip club, but the stage wasn't where she got the most attention or made her best tips. The well-dressed businessmen with fat wallets and corporate credit cards craved something more exotic than the hard-core biker broads they were force-fed over the years.

The kidnapped girl from Shanghai offered them something different. Perky natural breasts, the darker complexion that didn't come from a fake and bake, and a tiny frame that danced in their laps like a hummingbird. More than one client referred to her as a spinner; she thought it had something to do with ballet and her name, Tinkerbell.

The spinner learned that she could make much more money offstage, doing private dances in the VIP room. It meant putting up with lude comments and lots of groping, but Chen became proficient at the art of seduction, using teasing and alluring techniques to keep the cash flowing. Through hard-earned experience, she learned how to read men. She got to know who only wanted to play, and those who would pay.

Watching Chen dance, one would think she was actually trying to seduce her prey. The truth is she became a great actor, the queen bee. If they wanted to taste the honey, they had to pay her money. On a great night, she could make up to a thousand dollars in tips. The club always took their cut and some of it went to costumes and living expenses. Big Mike always left the club with a pocketful of her hard-earned cash.

The owners and management weren't stupid, and they knew what kind of money their peelers pulled in. They perched behind the bar like hawks spying their next meal. While working the floor and in their skimpy wardrobe, there weren't many places to hide their tips. Prying eyes and cameras were everywhere, and they weren't there to watch the customers.

The club even paid certain dancers to spy on the others, following them into the bathroom and changing room where there were no cameras. Chen had an ace in the hole with Mike, he was usually privy to who the rats were. The predators weren't the horny men who came into the club, but just about everyone else.

Tinkerbell had gained a following; regulars who made a point of sitting close to the stage when she was on and requesting private dances when she wasn't. The men weren't all executives and suits, there were guys like Gordon, a shy and lonely momma's boy who mostly wanted to talk, and asked her out to dinner more than once.

Pre-arranged sex in a motel or at their house was the only activity allowed outside the club. Ling, or one of the doormen, escorted them to the doctor's office and when they shopped for clothes. Chen lucked out once, when Mike was her escort. He showed her some of the city and the bank where he'd been stashing her money. The big man was the only true friend she had in the world.

Chen Shen's life was miserable, but she learned to cope, making it almost bearable. One night, after a grueling twelve-hour shift in the club, the doorman drove her to a nearby motel. He said some businessmen were having a party, celebrating a company merger, and they requested her presence as entertainment.

It wasn't an unusual request. Chen had danced at private parties before. Once in the room, she recognized two of the men as club patrons. One of them commented how she looked tired and offered her a line of coke. It was not something she liked to paid for, but she did it on occasion for a pick-me-up or extra energy.

Not being a much of a drinker, she refused a cocktail, but agreed to an orange juice. Shortly after her arrival, someone turned the music up. A man she'd never seen before grabbed her arm and tried to dance with her. A different guy told him to let her be. It wasn't her kind of dancing.

Tinkerbell knew that was her cue. She downed the OJ and started moving to the music. It wasn't her type of tune; the beat was too fast to keep in rhythm. One man said she didn't know how to dance and should just take her clothes off. The dancer set the pace and waited for the next song to take her blouse off. A couple men shouted for more.

After slipping her skirt off and dancing in her Victoria's Secret underwear, Chen felt lightheaded. She thought it was probably the cocaine fighting her fatigue for dominance. Her vision and mind went fuzzy. There were hands removing her remaining clothes. Bits of dark and light and more hands and gropes flashed through her mind. She heard pieces of music and shouts and laughter. Before Chen could figure out what was happening to her, everything went quiet and black.

When Miss Shen awoke, she was in the back of a truck with a dozen other women. She searched their faces and tried to focus, but didn't recognize any of them. One appeared vaguely familiar. She might have been in the truck on the way to Montreal. Was she dreaming? Was she ever in Montreal? It all seemed surreal. If she was there, why was she leaving and where was she going now? Her head hurt and thinking about it all made her dizzy.

She was laying in the prone position, with an arm draped over her duffle bag. Someone must have packed it for her. She couldn't remember going back to the house. The inside of her arm was tender and Chen noted a puncture mark. Someone had stuck her with a needle. She rolled onto her back and tried to sit up for a better look at herself.

Pain shot up from her buttocks and into her lower stomach. From what she felt, Chen knew she suffered from vaginal and anal trauma. What happened to her, and why couldn't she remember it? Her last memory was arriving at the hotel for a private dance. Her pain turned to nausea, and Chen rolled back onto her side. Fighting the urge to vomit, she wrapped herself around her duffle bag and cried.

Forty-Eight

Lady in Red

Beers and Wings were in order after the successful raid at Morneau's place, and being a team player, I had to partake. It just so happened both those things were in my favorite food groups. Back in my big eating days when they were five cents each, someone challenged me to eat fifty chicken wings. They would be paid for if I succeeded, but I would be stuck with the bill if not. I ate for free that night.

After the married cops went home, and the crowd thinned, I asked King if he wanted to hit the T & A strip club with me. Catching his surprised expression, I used the excuse that I needed to check in with Roxanne. The truth; I wasn't ready to call it a night, and there was no reason for me to rush home to an empty house. King said he'd pass; he was wiped out, and had a long ride home. We finished our drinks and headed off in separate directions.

On the drive, I couldn't help but wonder what my wife was up to. *Was she happier being on her own? Was she seeing anyone else, or had she called it off with her lover?* I pictured the two of them together. Someone behind me honked when I didn't move on the green light. I shook my head and told myself, out-loud, to stop thinking about it. It was something I picked up in a Dr. Phil or some other self-help book I'd recently purchased and read to help me cope. The challenge of trying to figure it all out seemed hopeless. Maybe it was time to move on.

The parking lot at the strip club was near full when I pulled in. There was a spot in the back row, far enough away from potential drunk drivers, so I parked there. Thinking for a second, I decided to call Roxanne. It went straight to voicemail. I left my car and went into the club.

Normally, I would have used my badge to avoid paying the cover charge, but I wanted to remain incognito and pulled out my wallet. The doorman held up his hand, signaling he didn't want my money. He tilted his head for me to proceed. I wasn't sure if he was being generous or recognized me as a cop. It really didn't matter.

Hanging just inside the doorway for a minute, I let my eyes adjust to the dark room. A young girl asked to take my coat but I declined and kept it on. The club was busy, with most tables filled, and pervert row lined up shoulder to shoulder. There were only two people seated at the bar. Judging by their attire and heavy war paint, I guessed they were off-duty peelers.

Bellying up to the opposite end of the bar, I ordered a drink and turned around to take in the action. There were at least ten strippers working tables of men, and a lot more Asians than the last time I'd been there. Two were pretending to have sex with each other on stage, something more risqué than I'd ever seen in a club.

The bartender tapped on my shoulder and pointed to my change. He mouthed something but I couldn't hear a word he said over the loud music. I barely had the money back in my pocket when an Asian peeler, who looked no more than sixteen, stopped in front of me. She quickly moved on when I shook my head and waved her off.

There were a few non-Asian dancers in the room but I didn't see Roxanne among them. The mystery resolved when the DJ announced Roxy was next up on stage. Realizing I'd sucked back my mixed drink already, I signaled the bartender for another, but in a tall glass. I drank everything fast and knew the extra pop would slow me down. To stretch it out even further, I liked to chew on the ice.

Staying put on my barstool I shooed away another stripper, one with cocaine eyes and more tattoos than an old sailor. Roxy strutted onto the stage as if she was a guest on The Tonight Show. Private Dancer by Tina Turner was her first song. She wore a short black sequin dress that looked painted on. It got my attention.

It was perfect. I'd never listened to all the words in the song, but it was written with exotic dancers in mind. The loud music vibrated through me and I watched how gracefully Roxy moved on stage. It was the most seductive dance I've ever seen. It wasn't just me. Men with other strippers already at their tables had their eyes glued on the woman in black.

Like a snake shedding its skin, Roxy slipped out of the dress for her second song. She wore a lacy red bra and panties, with a matching silk scarf. I had never paid a lot attention to the entertainment in my previous visits to strip clubs, but my informant's erotic performance had me mesmerized.

By the last song, Roxy wore nothing but the red silk scarf, strategically wrapped around her to keep the mystery and seduction alive. By far, it was the best sexual teasing I'd ever seen. Most other strippers simply danced to the music, shed their clothes, and then flaunted their body parts for everyone to see. For extra tips, some dancers smothered front row patrons with their breasts.

I didn't smoke, but when my CI left the stage, I felt like I needed a cigarette. I ordered another drink to cool off, and then someone slid onto the empty stool beside me. Roxanne must have spotted me when she was dancing. Not knowing what to say, I took a big gulp of my drink.

She leaned in so I could hear her. "Did you enjoy the show, Copper?"

"Uh...yeah, you could say that. You gave a whole new meaning to Tina's Private Dancer. I always thought she was pretty hot."

I stopped short of saying the same about her. It didn't seem right. Roxanne knew men and saw right through me. She played me some more.

"So, do you like the red lingerie or the black I had on last time you saw me?"

I hardly ever blush but felt I was, and knew she saw it too.

"Um...I don't normally like red...maybe it's how you present it." I tried to backpedal. "You chose the perfect music; I really like Tina Turner."

"You said." She smiled. "Okay, I'll stop fucking with you...I know you're not a paying customer, but I owed you that, after you hung up on me the other day. What brings you in to my part of the world tonight?"

I felt myself cooling down and regaining my composure. Being turned on like that surprised me, especially in a strip club, with someone I knew. Maybe I needed to get laid.

"Sorry, I felt bad about that but I had lots going on and you caught me at a busy time. I did try to call you back."

"No sweat, Storm, we're good."

"Cool. Hey, I see a lot of Asian women in here tonight...new talent?"

"New faces, but I wouldn't call them talent. Some couldn't dance if you shot bullets at their feet. Another group just came in today. They're shipping them in from affiliated clubs up in Montreal. I've lost a few regulars already...must be a novelty thing...half of them can't even speak English. They jerk guys off in the VIP room and fuck them off-sight. I'm not gonna compete with that, I do have some morals."

I glanced around to see if anyone else was close enough to hear our conversation.

"They're one of the reasons I'm here, the Morality guys are looking into this new Asian connection, seeing if it's above board. They've had complaints, I guess."

"What's the other reason?"

"Huh...oh...to see you of course."

"You're married, remember?"

I didn't get the chance to answer. A doorman interrupted and told Roxanne she was requested for a private dance. She glanced at me and shrugged.

"Duty calls. I'll catch ya later, hon."

My drink was empty and I considered another but thought not. After getting back into my car, I dialed Sandra's number. The fact she answered and said it was okay to come over, meant ex-sex was next on my agenda.

Forty-Nine

Sin City

It was as if Chen's life was repeating itself. The sad and distraught expressions on the other women's faces, and even the anxious horny clients, all started to look the same. The destinations were all similar. The innocent little girl from Shanghai had become a flesh commodity; a pleasure unit whose sole purpose was for someone else's profit. She was being moved around the world, by land and sea, to service rich businessmen and lonely working stiffs.

Chen no longer saw any light at the end of the tunnel. She knew the thought of returning home one day was only a pipe dream. Her future was as dim as the motel rooms she visited and the clubs where she danced. The new city was the same as the old city, even the flophouse looked the same.

The syndicate who operated the prostitution ring ran it like a private corporation. There were obviously men at the top whom Chen would never know, with the possible exception of Mr. Wong. She felt he had something to do with the business end of things. Everything ran like clockwork. Girls came and went, shuffled around without notice.

They kept them scared and confused enough to never ask questions. Their identification was out of reach and any money they were lucky enough to accumulate was taken. Ripped off once again, Chen arrived at her new home banged up and penniless. The ploy was used to keep the women in line.

The new club was the same as the old club; music, men, and money. One dancer called their new home Sin City. Another said it was tagged Tijuana of the North. None of it mattered to Chen. She did her job and tried to keep a glimmer of hope alive in her soul; the dream she might be able to escape it all someday.

Her new home was the T & A Gentleman's Club. Chen found nothing gentlemanly about the place and thought it lacked even more class than her last strip bar in Montreal. The manager's name was Rick and he was a dick. He commanded her and the other girls as if they were dogs in training. The local dancers didn't treat these new faces much better.

She'd seen it in the other clubs, where regulars got jealous when the new Asian girls drew more attention from customers. The only thing Chen liked about starting over in a new place, if there was anything worth liking, was how she could watch and learn from different seasoned dancers. She had grown quite adept at mimicking some of their moves. The better she got the more cash she made.

Chen couldn't help but wonder about the money she stashed away with Big Mike. Was that a write-off too? She couldn't pick up the phone and call him. Chances of her getting to one were slim to none, and even if she did, she didn't know his whole name or phone number.

There was no landline in the flophouse, and the girls weren't allowed to have cell phones. Even if Chen was able to use such a device, she had no idea who to call. Her family never had a telephone at home and Mike had been her only friend. One of the girls was caught making a call from the club in Montreal. They made sure not to leave marks, and only broke the fingers she dialed with so she could still perform.

Chen was just finishing a private dance in the VIP room at T & A one night, when she saw one of the locals start her show. The DJ called her Roxy, and played Private Dancer. The woman took to the stage as if she owned it. Chen found a dark corner to take a break, and watched the stage performance. The woman had short black hair and a nice figure for someone who appeared twice her age.

She wore a black sequin dress, hung low on her shoulders, and cut even lower to show her cleavage. The outfit was clingy and sparkly and the sexiest dress Chen had ever seen. She wore six-inch stilettoes but moved as if she was in flats. In awe, the Asian stripper watched the woman who reminded her of the ballerina she always wanted to be.

The white woman had skills. Roxy switched gears with the music and peeled down to sexy red lingerie and a matching scarf. Chen had learned to turn herself off when on stage, but this woman took it to a higher level. She was all about the tease, seducing men in the audience, willing them to throw money at her like confetti.

Even while naked wearing only the scarf, the woman oozed class and charm and charisma, all at the same time. She knew exactly what the men craved, but only gave them a taste so they'd beg for more. Horny clients lined up at the DJ booth, requesting private dances even before her stage show ended. Chen was so mesmerized she didn't notice the man standing beside her, trying to get her attention.

Later, after the grand finale, when all the girls were in the changing room at the same time, Chen approached Roxy and complimented her on her dance routine. The woman said thanks but turned away to dismiss her. She expected nothing more, but before the dancer walked away, Chen asked if Roxy could teach her someday. Roxy carried on as if she didn't hear the comment, offered the Asian a quick see-you-later wave, and left the room.

Fifty

Illegal Immigrants

With a bit of a thick head, I mumbled good morning at the boss' door on my way by. I was surprised he beat me in but remembered I was later than usual. Jim West grinned as I brushed past his desk, and I wondered if he could smell the previous night's booze on me. Making my way to my desk at the back of the office, I managed a couple more greetings to bodies who arrived ahead of me.

My lower back complained when I stuffed my gym bag under the desk and I wondered why my body was so sore. The ex-sex was good but I couldn't be that out of shape. I convinced myself it was the booze. It did more than kill a few brain cells. The word hangover wasn't in my vocabulary until I hit forty. Perhaps I was being punished and making up for all those years of liver abuse.

The message light on my phone was flashing, and a stack of files and paper filled my incoming tray; a normal morning. I checked my email and saw a list of messages and follow-ups. Yes, the world went on without me, nothing new there.

I saw that King started the morning count in my absence. "Thanks for getting into the overnights, Mike, you're my hero."

"No problem, boss, I figured you might be feeling a bit rough this morning. You were on a mission last night. Did you hook up with Roxanne?"

Before I could answer, Kevin Bell popped his head out of Gamble's office and waved me over. I needed food in my stomach and really hoped to get out for breakfast, but I waved back. I unlocked my desk, grabbed my journal, and headed to the boss' office.

Gamble's gaze locked onto mine. "Jesus Christ, Norm, what does it look like from your side of those bloodshot eyes?"

Bell chuckled and didn't say anything. He was a reformed alcoholic who'd been there and done much worse. Years earlier in Michigan, on one of his drunken benders, he lost track of a whole weekend. To his surprise and dismay, he was arrested for stealing a police car from a cop party he attended. It cost him big time, but he was able to keep his job.

"What's up boss? Sorry...I was actually out doing police work last night. After our successful raid...and uh, a few beers, I went to see my CI at the T & A."

I could see Bell was trying to stifle a laugh.

Gamble nodded along while he contemplated what I was trying to tell him.

"That's why we called you in...we want to take this thing up a notch...maybe put a task force together to investigate what's going on over there." He furled his brow and pursed his lips. "Why don't we take this down the street to Timmies...I could use a coffee, and you need to get something in your stomach to soak up the booze. The fresh air will do you good."

We reconvened down the street at the dead hockey player's coffee shop. Gamble was right. The brisk air cleared some of the cobwebs in my head. I ordered my usual toasted bagel and cream cheese, but with double bacon. I was never a coffee drinker and ordered an orange juice for the vitamin C. I stuffed my face while the boss sipped his coffee.

Bell leaned in so as not to share our conversation. "I spoke to Immigration and they want in. They've had complaints of undocumented illegals coming in from Asia, going to work in Toronto sweatshops, and in strip clubs from here to Kingston and Montreal. They don't have any undercover experience and are limited in their methods of investigation. When I reached out, they suggested we take the lead."

Gamble grasped his coffee cup with both hands and hunched over it as if trying to capture its heat. "Did your informant give you anything useful last night, Norm?"

"Not much...except to say they just got a batch of new arrivals, and the Asians are stealing business from the locals. She did add they're giving hand-jobs in the VIP room."

"I ran the task force idea up the flagpole. As usual, if we can have outside agencies foot most of the bill and provide manpower, they're all for it."

Bell and I exchanged glances. We'd been there before, the brass wanting a big bang without spending big bucks.

"I'm not sure how much my CI can give us. It's the slopes versus the round-eyes in there right now. The Asians are making money and the locals are jealous they're losing it."

eye, and waved me over to her table. I sat down
leaned in to talk over the music.

ok a little rough around the edges today."

probably drank a bit more than I should have last

you had a pretty good buzz going when you got

ne when I left."

because I told the bartender to cut back on the
our drinks."

oud of herself, she chuckled.

g about what she did, I should have been of-
I had to admit it was a good idea. "Thanks, mom,
ne's looking out for me."

ok happier today...did you get laid after you left
ight?"

the chick in the tutu, on stage? She's got some of
s..."

...can you believe it? Tinkerbell...the little nip-
ng me."

ipper? You need to come to my sensitivity train-
at work. That's why I popped in, actually..."

m not sensitive enough?"

ne of a kind, Roxanne, don't change on my ac-
, can you take a break? I need to talk to you
thing but this ain't the place to do it."

n slow and the manager's out. I'll tell the bar-
going out for a coffee. He'll be happy as long as I
ne."

led for the Tim Horton's down the street. I filled
ut my meeting earlier in the day. I explained
sk force to look into the immigration situation

Kevin Bell looked out the window; I could almost hear
the wheels turning in his head. "Do you think your girl
would be willing to dig deeper and testify down the road?
Maybe become an agent and come on the payroll? I'm sure
Immigration would foot the bill."

I thought about it. One of the General Squad Detectives
slid into the empty chair beside Gamble, effectively inviting
himself to our table. We called him Huge Head, for his abnormally large noggin. He was a good guy, but not known
for his stealth approach or ability to keep quiet.

The Human Head worked with Bell in the past and immediately struck up a conversation on a completely unre-
lated topic. I took the opportunity to bail and got up from
the table. Brian Gamble excused himself and told me to
wait up. I thought we'd pick up the work-related conversation on the walk back, but he asked about my home life instead.

Fifty-One

Playing Nice

Because of staff shortages, Roxanne had to work the day shift at T & A. She didn't mind, the clientele was completely different when the sun was up. Businessmen came in for liquid lunches and she had more time to work the room and do her thing. It didn't really interfere with her other job. She also worked from home as a bookkeeper.

One of her clients owned a small chain of submarine sandwich shops. Roxanne had always been good with numbers and took accounting in her last year of high school. The shop owner was crying in his beer one night at the club, after getting into trouble with Revenue Canada. Roxanne listened and offered a solution to the man's tax problem. Curious, and without a proper accountant, he invited her by his west side store one night to have a look at the books.

Impressed by her knowledge of business accounting, he gave her a shot at rectifying his predicament. After getting back in the good graces of the government, the business owner gave her the books for his other two stores. The sub shop owner didn't pay her much, but it was enough to start building a retirement fund so she could get out of the danc-

with the Asians, the prostitution in and around the club, and their possible connection to organized crime. I let her get some coffee and a couple Timbits into her system before I asked her about becoming an agent.

"How does that work? I'm already giving you information."

I explained the difference between an agent and a confidential informant. As an agent, she'd have to testify in open court. Before she could object too loudly, I added the part about getting a monthly salary for her help in the investigation.

"Testify? I dunno, Storm...it's no secret I'm a stripper...but I don't want to do it forever or have the whole world know about it...and if Rick and his partners are mobbed up, they could come after me."

"I know. It's not an easy ask. But it could also be a chance at a new start somewhere else. We could help you move and get another job. You've told me, more than once, there's nothing keeping you here Windsor."

"I know, but...I've got the bookkeeping gig now and I'm on the list to get into the methadone program here. Sounds like more stress in my life. What exactly, would I have to do?"

"Not much more than what you're doing now. Get friendly with your new stalker and get the inside scoop on the Asian girls. If she came down from Montreal, we might gain some insight into the operation up there. Maybe become one of Rick's rats, tell him the new girls are ripping him off somehow and you can keep an eye on them for him."

Roxanne ate another sugar-coated donut hole and washed it down with coffee while she thought about my offer. I sipped on my Diet Pepsi and gave her some time.

"I'll think about it, Storm. It's a lot to ask, but I can use the money and maybe even a fresh start somewhere else if you can promise I'll be safe."

"I won't make you any promises until the powers that be put it in writing for you, and I'm convinced you'll be okay. You have my word on that."

Fifty-Two

The China Syndrome

It took more than a week to get everyone together who wanted to be on board with our task force. Someone dubbed it *The China Syndrome*. Unlike the movie about a nuclear meltdown kept secret, our goal was to uncover an organized crime syndicate involved in a sex trafficking operation spanning two continents.

Canada Immigration was interested from the get-go, and since their end of it was a federal matter, they suggested we bring the Mounties into the mix. As it turned out, the RCMP was already looking into a shipping and smuggling operation in conjunction with the Montreal Police. At my suggestion, since we had complaints about communicable diseases among the Asian women, I invited a friend from the Health Department.

The first meeting took place in the project room across the hall from the Street Crimes office. A secretary from Investigations was there to take notes. The Inspector in charge of the division graced us with his presence, mostly to hear the Mounties would fund the task force. I knew we wouldn't see him again until the project's conclusion if and when the media cameras showed up.

Staff Sergeant Gamble used the Street Crimes slush fund to spring for coffee and donuts and we spent the first half hour doing introductions and getting to know each other. I liked my boss; he included diet pop for me. Sergeant Bell and I suggested Gamble run the show and see where the cards fell when we got underway.

He began by explaining what was going on in two strip clubs we knew about locally. Exotic dancers from China were shipped to Montreal, Kingston, Niagara Falls, and Windsor. A few nods from some around the table told me we weren't in a unique situation. Gamble explained how the foreign dancers were committing certain sex acts in the clubs and prostituting themselves in nearby hotels. He added the Morality Unit received anonymous complaints the women were also passing on communicable diseases such as gonorrhea and herpes.

My friend, Carrie Smith, from the Board of Health, con- firmed the uptick in those and other STDs within the Wind- sor's region. Because of confidentiality rules, she couldn't provide any personal details at that point in the investiga- tion. She said her superiors were aware of the situation and they were in the process of seeking opinions from their le- gal eagles.

Bell reported on what he and his team had been able to uncover in the clubs thus far and referred to me to fill in the group about an agent we had working in the T & A Gentle- men's Club. Roxanne had come in earlier in the week and signed the agreement. She was still afraid of repercussions down the road, but the one thousand dollar a month salary we offered helped convince her it was worth the risk.

We also had one of our guys from Intelligence on the team. The unit monitored organized criminal factions like the Chinese triads. He and the Mountie from their Organized Crime Section enlightened us. The Asians were linked to strip clubs in Canada. According to them, everything tied into their shipping and smuggling operations.

He said Interpol took down a similar operation in Europe. Truckloads of hijacked electronics from China were shipped to and sold in Germany, France, and Belgium. During one of their raids, police discovered a truck full of young Chinese women, apparently destined for the sex trade.

Gamble asked if we should try to get Interpol on board with our task force. The Mountie said he didn't think it was necessary so early in our investigation, but he would reach out to a contact there for any updated information. I sat back in my chair and took in the variety of law enforcement experience in the room. It was my belief we were onto something big, but in considering the logistics involved, I had to wonder how far we'd get.

My boss started around the table, assigning specific tasks. The secretary interrupted him. She said she needed to change the tape, and he took the opportunity to suggest a break. Separate conversations broke out amongst the group and I pulled the Intelligence guy aside to ask if my buddy, Shadow, was in his office.

I made my escape and headed to the Intelligence office. I had some concerns about Roxanne and thought about how we could keep her safe during and after the conclusion of our project. Shadow was on a panel with other Canadian Police agencies who oversaw our version of Witness Protection, and I thought it best to run things by him before my CI got into it neck deep.

Fifty-Three

BFFs

Tinkerbell continued to copy and mimic Roxy's dance moves, and instead of getting angry, the older and more experienced woman accepted it as a compliment. It's not as if she patented her routine. Now that she was receiving payment for it, Roxanne paid more attention to the young Asian, and went out of her way to be friendlier.

Chen ate it up like birthday cake. She didn't have any friends and felt special to warrant the attention of a local and experienced dancer like Roxy. The seasoned dancer broke the ice in the locker room by revealing her real name, and suggesting the young dancer come to her with any problems she might have at the club.

She was a private person, and normally a bit shy, but Chen felt comfortable around Roxanne. Maybe it was because she missed her mother so much and didn't have any other mature females who she could look up to. If she needed a mentor or role model in her life, her new friend fit the bill.

One night the two women found themselves working the same table of businessmen. The rowdy group of six warmed up with lots of shots, taking turns chatting with Roxy and Tinkerbell, and passing them from lap to lap. Waitresses knew the routine whenever clients bought the girls drinks, they simply told the bartender which dancer they were for, and the appropriate non-alcoholic or mixed concoction was served.

The ruse normally worked, but one of the men was drinking wine and passed glasses off to the women. It wasn't a problem for Roxanne, who could handle her booze, and liked wine. It was different for Chen, who had consumed only watered-down wine in the past while trying to play the role. The group of suits hung onto the women until Roxy was called to the stage. Tinkerbell left at the same time, saying she needed to use the bathroom.

The rambunctious crowd kept all of the dancers busy all night. By last call, only two of the table of six businessmen remained. There were half-drank and full glasses of wine on the table that they insisted the girls drink before they went to waste. Both Roxanne and Chen showed signs of impairment, with the latter a bit wobblier.

After the doorman kicked out the remaining suits, the two dancers took their glasses to a dark table in the corner. They shared personal and private things, but Roxanne wasn't ready for what she was about to hear. Chen spilled her guts and told her new confidant how her life changed the day she was kidnapped from her home in Shanghai, China.

The young Asian's glassy eyes watered as she laid out her tale of woe; how she was sold into the sex trade. The alcohol caused Chen to slur her words, but the sentences she formed were like spears that pierced Roxanne's heart. In all her life, she had never heard such a sad and horrific story.

She raised a hand to catch a tear rolling down her cheek, and slid her chair closer to Chen to put an arm around her. The girl, who Roxanne affectionately dubbed Little China Doll, broke down and bawled. It was the first time she cried that hard, since the day they kidnapped her.

All the lounge lights switched off, except for one behind the bar and those at the emergency exits. The bartender called out and pointed the women to their change room. Roxanne offered a shoulder to Chen, who was drunk and couldn't walk. She paused to kick off her six-inch heels. It helped, but she collided with a doorframe.

The older dancer guided her young protégé to a chair, and told her to stay put while she slipped into a pair of track pants and her jacket. Normally, one of the doormen walked the girls across the alley to their house, but they had all left for the night. Roxanne wrapped Chen's coat around her shoulders, and practically carried her to the door.

It took forever to find her keys to get in the rear entrance. Her mentor took over after she fumbled with the lock. On autopilot, Chen led the way into the house and up the stairs. It was quiet with most everyone asleep, but Roxanne heard moaning and caught a glimpse through a partially open door, of someone having sex.

Another half open door revealed four women sleeping on two mattresses on the floor. When they got to Chen's room it was no different, and she practically fell into the only empty spot available, beside another female. There were four women in the room, sharing two beds. Roxanne was stunned. She froze for a moment, taking it all in.

In her car on the way home, Roxanne thought about what she'd seen in the house where Chen lived. It was un-believable. She flashed back to her own early years, when her mom's boyfriend started kissing and groping her, trying to have sex. Mothers were supposed to protect their daughters but she blamed it on her, saying she was trying to seduce him, and maybe she should try living with her father.

Roxanne did exactly that, and her dad didn't mind having her stay with him. He was a long-distance trucker who was hardly ever home. His absence led to her staying out and hanging with the wrong crowd. She acted out, shoplifted, and tried various kinds of drugs. A few years later her father found her passed out on the couch with a needle sticking out of her arm.

Coping with life and living on her own, only drove Roxanne further down the rabbit hole. She shacked up with friends and bounced from job to job, eventually landing a gig as a shooter girl in a local strip bar. Roxanne soon realized the real money was in dancing. It actually looked better than what she was doing; wearing little more than the strippers and having men grope her all night while trying to carry a tray full of drinks.

Her life had been difficult, but she couldn't get what Chen told her out of her mind. Kidnapped, raped, and abused, since she was a child. And it was no better now; a sex slave forced into prostitution and dancing. How could she possibly live like that, sharing dirty mattresses and having people copulating right beside you in the same room? It was inhumane, to say the least.

Roxanne parked in the lot outside of her apartment building and reached in her coat pocket for her keys. She found a wad of money but waited until she was inside to check it out. There was at least five hundred dollars, but it wasn't hers. She replayed the night's events in her head. It had to belong to the China Doll.

Fifty-Four

The Info Flow

Roxanne held her coffee mug with both hands, and stared beyond it to the six hundred and fifty dollars she had spread out on the table. Because of the large bills, there was more money than she had thought. It wasn't the most money she'd ever seen but it was still a lot, enough for a new set of tires for her car, or maybe something nice for herself. She knew it wasn't her money and it had to be Tinkerbell's.

Why would she stuff it into her coat pocket? The woman was drunk and must have done it by mistake. Roxanne thought about the life story Chen shared with her. The kind of horror tale you only read about or watch on television. Maybe she didn't trust anyone and gave the money to her for safekeeping.

Roxanne took a sip of coffee, holding the cup to her chin to enjoy its warmth for a moment. Placing it back on the table she reached out and gathered the paper money into a pile. She gazed out the window at the gloomy sky and light snowfall, wondering what it would be like to go somewhere warm, like Cancun. Her phone rang but she ignored it and headed for the shower.

With another task force meeting set for the afternoon, I called Roxanne to check in and get an update from her. My call went directly to voicemail. I left a message asking her to get back to me as soon as she got the message. Bell gave me a wave from his desk, signaling he was ready to go. We arranged for a breakfast meeting and grabbed our boss on the way out the door.

Entering through the back door at Elias Deli, we paused to say a quick hello to Louie. I'd been craving his corned beef hash so I ordered a pile of it with a couple fried eggs thrown on top for good measure. The waitress, Connie, wore a permanent smile and called me by name each time she came to our table. Gamble commented he was happy I was back in action.

It took me a minute to get what he meant, but it went over Bell's head. He got right down to business, saying he wanted us to have our ducks in a row before the afternoon meeting. He thought the Mounties worked too slowly. Gamble rolled his eyes when Bell turned to me. Neither of us were surprised by his comments. He earned the moniker of Taz, for Tasmanian devil. He asked me if I'd heard from Roxanne. I said it was a bit early for her, and I left a message to get back to me ASAP.

Connie delivered our food and I tried to get a read on her. She was a pretty woman with a great body. I had known her for years, seeing her when I worked off-duty in the bars. Never seeing her with a man, I thought maybe she played for the other team.

Bell carried on, saying he and his guys were doing surveillance on T & A and the surrounding motels when they had time. With his limited manpower he admitted it was difficult to track women from the club, and prove they were soliciting in the motels.

Gamble said he could ask Uniform if they had any extra bodies to lend us. Bell washed down a mouthful of scrambled eggs with his coffee while he considered the offer of extra help.

I took advantage of him being indisposed for a moment.

"Do you remember my buddy, Ham, the guy who did the rub n' tug for us?"

Bell just shoveled another load of food into his mouth, but Gamble nodded. He raised his eyebrows and dabbed the corner of his mouth with a napkin.

"You want to use him for The China Syndrome?"

Bell sat back in his chair in thought. His wheels turned while he chewed and listened.

"Are you kidding? Free drinks and a blow-job on us...I'm sure he'd jump at the chance to do his civic duty."

Connie just put down another glass of diet cola for me and heard the sexual comment. She avoided eye contact, but I'm sure I caught her smirk before she turned away.

After a hard swallow, Bell leaned in towards me. "That could work." He eyed Gamble. "You think the horsemen will go for it? Do we really need to tell them?"

I knew the dilemma. There was a line that separated a confidential police informant from a police agent. When Ham visited the massage parlor and passed on the information, it was at his suggestion, which kept him in the informant category. If we specifically asked him to do it for us, he became our agent and accordingly, had to testify. Sometimes the line got blurred.

Gamble replied. "It's their money but as they say, it's easier to ask forgiveness than permission. Maybe we can just float the idea at the meeting to see what kind of reaction we get. In the meantime, Norm, maybe you can reach out and run it by your buddy. With his old lady ready to pop, he'll be looking for a little dickstraction."

He and Bell laughed. A swallow of pop slipped down my windpipe, and I almost spewed it across the table.

Fifty-Five

The Hangover

Terrified by the height, the mother and daughter clung to each other for support. The little girl was old enough, but an inch too short for the Ferris Wheel. The operator agreed to let her on the ride if the adult accompanied her. It was all Chen could talk about that summer, waiting for the carnival to arrive in town. Her mother was leery of heights but obliged for her daughter's sake.

The view from the top offered an amazing panorama of the Huangpu River and City of Shanghai. The metal car they were in rocked back and forth when the ride came to a stop and new riders got on at the bottom of the giant wheel. A seagull came so close; Chen thought she could reach out and touch it. It turned and flew straight into the sun.

The wheel lurched forward and their car began to descend, but Chen's sleeve caught on something. Her arm went next and she was lifted from her seat. Mrs. Shen tried to hold on but her daughter was pulled from her grasp. Chen screamed and tried to resist; her arm would be yanked from its socket. Extracted from the seat, she dangled in midair. The silhouette of the seagull appeared in front of the sun.

Another tug on her arm woke Chen up. One of the other women stood over her bed staring down at her. Opening her peepers was painful, as if her forehead was swollen and putting pressure on her eyelids. The woman said Rick wanted to see her at the club, right away. When Chen sat up the contents of her stomach sloshed around and she felt nauseous. Thinking she was about to vomit, the China Doll headed to the bathroom.

Seeing her bloodshot and sunken eyes in the mirror, and noting her dry mouth and upset stomach, Chen felt the effects of her first hangover. She remembered drinking wine with Roxanne and some clients, and drinking more wine later, but she couldn't recall leaving the club, or how she got home.

After splashing cold water on her face, and getting a few handfuls of it down her parched throat, Chen fixed her hair and returned to her room. Realizing she slept in her clothes and was still in them, she changed into a pair of sweats. The same woman who woke her up poked her head in the door and said she'd better hurry. Rick sounded pissed.

Dazed and a little dizzy, she stood in the middle of the room. Chen tried to remember what she did wrong. She thought she forked over the club's cut for the night. Money; she tried to remember what she did with her stash. Chen went through her clothes and checked her latest hiding place, a seam in the curtains. The previous night's money wasn't there. She checked two older hideouts but there was nothing.

The sad thing was Chen didn't even remember how much cash she had. In her drunken state, she wondered if maybe she hid it at the club, or dropped it on the way home. Grabbing a winter coat from a hook near the back door, she headed to the club. She checked both sides of the path and in the alley on the way, but didn't see any money laying around. Someone would have taken it anyway.

When she got to the office door, and reached out to knock, one of the doormen stepped out. It was Dave, the one she hated. He never had a nice word for her, and called all the Asian dancers Slants or Slopes. Sporting a toothy grin, he held the door for Chen, but barely wide enough for her to slip through the opening. He mumbled something but she couldn't hear what he said from inside the office.

She stood in silence in front of Rick's desk, while he tended to paperwork and purposely ignored her. He was an attractive man, with short brown hair and a matching goatee. Lifting his eyes from the ledger in front of him, he sighed and started into a spiel straight from a management handbook. He praised Chen for her hard work, long hours, and the good money she was making for the club.

The China Doll felt herself swaying while she stood and tried to focus on her boss. He got up and walked around his desk, stopping directly in front of her. He changed his tone and accused Chen of skimming profits belonging to him. That his take from her was consistently lower than the other dancers.

He chastised her for bringing an outsider into the house where she lived. It was not allowed, and she knew better. Rick placed a hand on her shoulder as if to comfort her, but instead he squeezed and dug his thumb into her collarbone. Chen winced and was about to tell him she had no idea how she got home.

As she opened her mouth to speak, Rick drove his fist into her stomach. The blow stole her breath and buckled her legs. Chen grabbed the leather chair in front of the desk on her way down. As her knees hit the floor, she threw up all over herself, the chair, and the plush carpet. She gasped to catch her breath.

Rick yelled for Dave, who must have been waiting outside the office. He rushed in and his boss told him to get the little whore out of his sight. The doorman grabbed Chen by the hair and pulled her towards the door. Rick shouted at him to make sure he came back and cleaned up her mess. He continued his rant, following them into the lounge, and telling Tinkerbell to get her ass back after she cleaned herself up. She was to work a double shift.

Fifty-Six

Stoked

I had just taken my seat in the project room, when Roxanne returned my call. Mouthing her name to Gamble and pointing to my phone, I left the room to answer the call. I gave her shit for taking so long to get back to me, but she ignored it, and filled me in on her new Asian friend, Chen, known in the club as Tinkerbell.

Bell poked his head out of the door to wave me in, but I held a hand up to let him know I'd be a few minutes. I could tell by Roxanne's tone and rapid-fire conversation she was excited and had news to report. Debating whether I should be writing stuff down, I took a few steps toward my office to grab a pad of paper.

My wife cut me off as I came around the corner. We still worked in the same building, but were on different floors and mostly isolated from each other. I uttered the words 'Asian strippers' to Roxanne on the phone. Sandra made eye contact with me. Seeing her quizzical expression, I simply smiled and waved.

She continued down the hall and I ducked into my office for paper. Roxanne's voice was in my ear but my wife was in my head. Comments from past discussions flashed through my brain, competing with the new information I was taking in. I found a pad on the closest desk. Sitting down to take notes, I quashed my negative thoughts.

After getting everything that I needed from Roxanne, I returned to the meeting across the hall. Bell filled in the group on his surveillance results around the T & A and neighboring motels. He said we had an informant working inside the club and he turned over the floor to me.

I gave a brief background about my CI, and told everyone I just got off the phone with her. Referring to what I already knew, and what Roxanne told me, I explained how my informant befriended one of the Asian dancers. According to the new source, as a child, she was kidnapped from her home in China to cover an outstanding family debt. They used her as forced labor for a while, before they raped and prostituted her.

The young woman said she and many others like her were stuffed into shipping containers, and transported to Montreal. Some stayed there to work in bawdy houses, and others in strip clubs. A couple girls died along the way and didn't make it to Canada. I went on, telling how the women stripped and prostituted themselves to pay their debts to the Triad. Any documentation they might possess was held as collateral.

My friend from the Health Department, Carrie Smith, sat beside me. She cleared her throat and when I glanced her way, it appeared she was about to cry. Our Mountie representative, Barney Stoker, spoke up and asked me pointed questions as to the identities of my informant and the Asian woman. I felt my temperature rise a few degrees while I politely listened to him.

Another horseman I knew from my days in the Drug Squad, told me Stoker was selected by CSIS (Canadian Security Intelligence Service), and on a personal mission to impress his new bosses. The agency was relatively new and still trying to find their place in the world of intelligence organizations. After a lackluster performance out of the gate, their new mandate including raiding key personnel from the RCMP, and building their informant base by any means possible.

I knew from personal experience, the Mounties paid incentive money to their sources in the hopes they dug up information. It was a great for some informants. They often supplied tips that were common knowledge on the street and collected money for the useless information.

I averted my eyes from Stoker for a second, and gave Gamble my best 'what the fuck' look. He interjected and suggested we slow things down a bit. My CI had just made contact inside the Asian circle. It was too early to push either woman too hard. Bell started to say something but Stoker cut him off.

He reminded us our informant was a police agent, financially supported by the China Syndrome task force, which in reality meant she was on the RCMP payroll. Stoker said the smuggling investigation in Montreal had stalled and they needed someone on the inside to connect the dots from continent to continent.

I leaned in, folded my arms in front of me on the table, and stared at the anxious horseman. Before he could open his mouth again, I told him the information I received was only hours old, and as in any other police investigation, we needed to look into it, and confirm what we could before taking any further action.

Bell pointed out we hadn't seen much of anything from further up the food chain, referring to the lack of information from the Mounties or Montreal Police. He said it would be nice if the task force was better informed before they pushed the agent in over her head. Gamble agreed with his Sergeant but suggested I try to get an introduction from our CI, to meet the Asian woman. I had already thought about that when on the phone with Roxanne, and openly expressed it to the room.

Carrie Smith reached in and touched my arm, signaling she wanted to say something. I told her to go ahead and she said her office noticed a recent uptick in reported STD's, and their follow-up inquiries pointed to the Asian connection. No one responded. It was as if she just told everyone around the table that they were infected.

Carrie blushed, feeling she embarrassed herself. Gamble came to her rescue and suggested her office look into it some more, trying to pinpoint the hotspots in the city. He said we might be able to use her information further down the road. Seeing Stoker wasn't satisfied and still chomping at the bit, my boss suggested we call it, a day.

Fifty-Seven

Double Agents

Ham normally answered directly or got right back to me when I reached out, but it wasn't until later that night when he called me back. It was late in the evening, and I was at home watching one of The Magnificent Seven movies; the one with Yule Brenner. My CI apologized for not getting back to me earlier, and said he was in the hospital all day with his girlfriend. She went into false labor.

I made light of it and said that's what happens when you can't keep your dick in your pants. Ham laughed and said he couldn't wait for it to be over. He actually looked forward to being a father. It was a boy and he said he thought about naming him after me but couldn't find a suitable Muslim name for Norm. We spent another couple of minutes poking fun at each other.

He knew I usually called for a reason. Trying not to task him directly, I asked if he ever went to the T & A strip club. Ham said it had been a while since he'd been there, but his brother was a frequent flyer and bragged about getting a hand-job from one of the girls there.

Ham chuckled. "Ah, I get it...you're looking into the peeler bar. But aren't you still in the B & E Squad?"

"Yeah, but I'm under the Street Crimes umbrella, with the Morality Unit. We team up sometimes...like the massage parlor, remember?"

"A happy ending as I recall."

We both laughed.

"It was, for everyone except the brothers we busted. Hey, do you know if the stripper your brother hooked up with was Asian?"

"Didn't say...he's practically a virgin, never had a steady girlfriend...I don't know what's the matter with him, I..."

"You know I can't ask you directly to get involved, but if you think there's a chance you might accompany your brother to the club one night...we could use another set of eyes in there."

"Another?"

"I can't get into it, but we know there's a group of Asian dancers in there now. Your brother is proof of what's going on in the VIP room, but we've also heard the girls are banging customers down the block at the local motels."

Ham didn't say anything for a few seconds while he thought about it. I grabbed the remote and turned down the volume for the upcoming gun battle. I'd seen the movie at least five times before.

"Sure, Norm, sounds like a good idea...my brother owes me birthday drinks."

"Happy belated. Give me a heads up before you go and I'll chip in for a round."

"Cool. Are you paying for me to get my nuts off this time too?"

I laughed. "The law works in mysterious ways."

"I think you mean the Lord."

"I thought you weren't religious...but yeah, we'll cover it, somehow. Let me know for sure so I can tell you what, and who, to look for at the club."

"No problem, Norm. I gotta go...the whale's calling me into the bedroom, and it ain't for sex."

"That's not very nice."

"Her words, not mine. Catch ya later."

Fifty-Eight

Still Hangin'

Chen suffered through the day, promising herself she'd never drink alcohol again. The bartender suggested a virgin bloody Mary, but she only threw it up. Someone else suggested the greasy chicken wings offered to the lunch crowd. It helped with her nausea, but the breaded meat weighed heavy in her stomach. She wished for a big bowl of her mother's pho.

She was happy to see the night shift. It meant a longer rotation, and gave her more down time. Chen was even more elated to see Roxanne, someone who she believed she could call a friend. The previous night's events were still lost in her foggy brain, but she did recall sharing much of her life story.

Once the day girls left, and most of the night crew had vacated the changing room, Chen cornered Roxanne. Only one other dancer remained in the room, but she got the hint when Tinkerbell and Roxy used their eyes to throw daggers at her. The older dancer wasn't sure why, but she hugged her new Asian friend. Chen winced.

"Are you okay? That looks like more than hangover pain."

"I'm never drinking wine again." She dropped her eyes. "Rick hit me...I think he bruised a rib."

"Oh my God! What a fucker...has he done that before?"

"Not to me, but he's hit the others...said I ripped him off, skimmed from their profits."

"I thought you gave them their cut last night..."

"Me too...and I think they took the rest of my money...I always hide some...but they must have found it."

"You gave it to me...$650. I found it in my coat pocket last night when I got home. You must have put it there when I walked you home."

"I got shit for that too. I don't remember giving you the money...or anything else, really. Thanks for taking care of me...I hope I didn't get you into trouble."

"I'm fine, don't you worry about me. Why would you get shit for me walking you home?"

"The rules say no outsiders are allowed in our house."

Roxanne snuggled up beside Chen on the bench and put an arm around her. "I saw why last night. They've got you caged like animals. One of the girls was having sex in the bedroom next to yours."

"That's not unusual. It's allowed for special clients...men involved in the organization."

"What organization?"

"The men who kidnapped and brought me here. I don't know much about them except how they all work together, using and moving us all over, making lots of money. I think the man I cleaned house for in China has something to do with it, but I've learned to cope and gave up trying to figure it out."

"That's crazy...it's human trafficking. We've got to figure out a way to get you out of this."

Chen's eyes glazed over, but she managed to hold back her tears. "That's why I gave you my money...I stash some away whenever I can...so maybe I can escape this life and go home. I miss my family every day."

"That's okay...I can hold it for you...you know you can trust me."

"I do, you're the only friend I have...except for Big Mike."

"Who?"

"He was a doorman at one of the Montreal clubs...he opened a bank account for me."

"That's great, maybe he can help us. What's his last name?"

A tear broke free from Chen's left eye and rolled down her cheek. She batted it away as if it was a pesky fly. "I don't know...they drugged and raped me, and pulled me out of Montreal before I could talk to him. He has my bankbook."

Roxanne broke eye contact as she teared up. She stared into empty space and shook her head in disgust.

"Those fuckers...I want you to meet a friend of mine...he's a police officer."

Chen's eyes grew wide and bulged. She shook her head violently.

"No police. Back home, they're worse than criminals. In Montreal, two came in to see the manager all the time. They used some of the girls for free." Chen shook her head again. She stood and faced Roxanne for a second, then turned and left the room.

Fifty-Nine

Crime Statistics

I was hip-deep in my morning paperwork when I saw Jim West walk in, balancing a tray of drinks in one hand and carrying a bag of goodies from Timmies in the other. It was my cue to join him, Bell, and Gamble in his office, for our monthly meeting of unit supervisors. After we all grabbed our morning wake-ups, the boss read us an at-a-boy, that came down from the top, congratulating us on a reduction in crime for the past month.

It was always about statistics for the bean counters, something I found amusing. It took me back to my uniform patrol days when computerization brought us out of the dark ages. With everything digitized, locations, and types of crimes could be easily tracked. Some thought certain trends could be predicted.

The Staff Sergeant in charge of my platoon at #2 Station firmly believed in what he called *directed patrol*; a new term used to target particular zones within the patrol districts. The boss brought my partner and me up on the carpet one day. He pointed out we needed to do more traffic enforcement in a certain zone in our district. When I inquired, he referred to the one hundred percent rise in fatal accidents in the area.

Puzzled, and trying to act genuinely interested, I examined his statistics. It was right there in black and white. There was one fatality in the past month and none the month before—a one hundred percent increase. My partner and I did our best not to laugh in front of the man we affectionately called Bing Bong, behind his back.

Sergeant West went first, bringing us up to speed on the Auto Squad. There wasn't much, except for an unusual spree of stolen construction machinery. East end building sites reported missing backhoes, bobcats, and even a bulldozer. He added no local suspects came to mind, and he put out feelers across Southern Ontario for similar occurrences.

Bell went next, reporting on the success of Morality's latest john sweep—a sting operation where female undercover officers lured any potential johns cruising the streets in search of prostitutes. Since the majority of our female cops looked better than the street hookers, it was like finding tall men on a basketball team. In some cases, potential johns lined up waiting.

Timing it perfectly, Roxanne called me just as Bell brought up The China Syndrome. I answered and told her I was in a meeting, adding she'd be on a phone speaker, so she could update others involved in the project who were in the room.

She sounded a bit groggy. I assumed she worked the night shift.

"Storm...and whoever else is listening...this thing is way bigger than you think. I'm not sure how much I can help, Chen says some kind of crime syndicate is running the show from here to China, and there are cops involved. I'm not sure this is what I signed up for."

Not being on the task force, West flipped his brow and quietly asked Bell who Chen was.

Roxanne heard him and continued. She sounded wound up.

"Chen is my new friend...one of the Asian dancers you wanted me to get close to. She said she trusts me and gave me some of her money. Rick beat her up and I saw what goes on in the house where all the girls stay...men are fucking the women right there; I couldn't believe it. It's a flop house where they have to share dirty mattresses...I've never seen anything like it."

The four of us exchanged horrified looks.

I spoke up while Roxanne took a paused. "Okay, take a couple deep breaths and slow down."

I heard a slurping noise, as if she took a sip of coffee.

"Her life is a shit-show, Storm...she keeps telling me stuff...like a doorman who is holding money for her in Montreal. She wants to escape so I told her she should meet you but she freaked out when I said you were a cop."

"Hang on, what did she say about cops being involved?"

"In Montreal...two who came into the club all the time and got freebies from the girls. She just thinks police are bad everywhere. I don't know what to do now...I might have scared her off. Where are you guys at with this thing?"

I took in the faces of Bell and Gamble. The boss held his hands up and pushed the air, a signal for me to slow her down so we could regroup.

"It's okay, Roxanne, stay calm. Give it some time, and see if Chen comes back to you. By the sound of it, she has nobody else she can trust. Wait her out but stay close, and show her you support her no matter what. We've got a few things in the works here. Hang tight and I'll get back to you later."

She sighed. "All right, Storm, I think I need to get high now."

Sixty

Monday Off

It was my long weekend. I was off Saturday, Sunday, and Monday. I went out for boy's night on Friday, and I spent most of the next day nursing my hangover. While catching up on a few days' worth of newspapers, I gazed at the gloom in my back yard. Everything was dead or asleep for the winter. The evergreen cedars along the north side of my property offered the only splash of color.

Even my fish were sleeping. A thin layer of ice covered the pond and everything below it appeared to be in suspended animation. I considered going back to bed, but got into a movie-watching marathon instead. At one point, I got bored and surfed an online dating site to see what prospects my future might hold.

On Sunday, I took my mother out for breakfast. Bored as well, she asked what color combination I wanted for my knitted Christmas present. Mom went through her own breakup when I was eleven. She shared a secret story with me, and asked why my wife left her cat behind. That afternoon I wondered the same thing.

Why was the feline my problem? Sandra can't have pets in her apartment? Thinking about the cat and our separation got me pissed off. I threw the cat in its cage, drove into the city, and left the furry little bitch at Sandra's door. It was just as well she wasn't home. I was more sarcastic in my phone message than I would have been in person.

I felt energized Monday morning. I ate a light breakfast and headed to the gym in Kingsville. Before I could exit my car, I fielded a call from Ham.

"Hey, I wasn't sure if you were on days or nights and didn't want to bother you on your weekend off."

"It's my three-day weekend...I'm headed into the gym. What's up?"

"I met my brother at the T & A Saturday night, I thought..."

"You were supposed to call me first."

"I know, I know...it wasn't planned. He drank too much and called me to pick him up."

"I thought it was against your religion for you guys to drink?"

"We don't believe in that shit...except for the pork thing. No offense."

"You're funny. None taken. So?"

"Yeah, you were right. I only stayed for one drink but the place was crawling with Chinese pussy. My brother said the peeler who gave him the hand-job wasn't there. I tried to chat one up but she wanted money just to talk to me. I took a peek in the VIP room to see what was going on, but a bouncer turned me around. I didn't have the extra cash for that game."

"Anything else?"

"No that's it...but I told my brother what you're looking for. He knows I work for you and is cool with it since you helped him with that traffic ticket."

"All right. I'm heading into the gym right now so I'll get back to you later."

I ended the call and went to work out. While flat on my back and trying to crunch away my bulging waistline, my gym bag rang. It was easier to roll over to reach it than getting up. It was my brother Willy's stepdaughter, Lisa. I let the call go to voicemail and would get back to her later. The workout felt good; my chest and shoulders felt pumped. When I hit the first leg machine, my phone rang again. It was Roxanne. She was on the way into work and wanted to know if I had any special instructions for her.

Catching my reflection in the wall mirror, I noted the little smile. *What was that saying...in for a penny, in for a pound?* Roxanne was in, committed to her new role as a police agent. I knew the money motivated her, but obviously, she was also on a mission to save her new Asian friend. I thanked her for checking in, explained where I was, and told her to get back to me later.

Having lost all momentum, I barely broke a sweat finishing my workout. The grocery store was right across the street and my next stop. With only a few items in my shopping cart, I wasn't surprised when my phone rang again.

Carrie Smith politely asked how my Monday morning at work was going. A telling edge in her voice said she had something for me. I didn't bother to mention it was my day off. I flashed back to the party where I met Carrie for the first time. Blonde hair, eyes the color of milk chocolate, and a body begging to be explored. I was happily married at the time, but smitten with her fresh looks and bubbly personality. Working as a city Meter Maid, she was a friend of my car partner.

From parking enforcement, she moved to social services, and eventually to the Health Department. Now I was single, thoughts about hooking up with her rushed through my head. I couldn't help it. We always had what I considered a flirtatious relationship, but my marital status was a barrier keeping us at bay. That, and the fact she was probably too young for me. It was wishful thinking on my part.

Carrie told me she looked deeper into the surge of reported STD's and found some alarming patterns. She said her office had difficulty in tracing infection sources, because the male patients offered very little information about their possible contacts. But enough of them believed female prostitutes infected them, and more specifically, the Asian strippers from the T & A.

According to my hot friend, tracking sources in the case of prostitutes, who used fake names and addresses, made it next to impossible to trace infections to their origin. Privacy laws made it even worse. She said they got lucky when statistics from a certain clinic on the west side showed an outbreak of serious STDs within a small group of Asian women. Carrie said the clinic could not legally provide names, but they mentioned the infected women were all in the entertainment industry.

I wasn't sure how any of this new information was going to help our task force. Barney Stoker questioned my friend's involvement from the get-go, and I had wondered if he was right. A feeling told me she was on to something.

While I stored her report in the right side of my brain, the left side wanted to ask Carrie out. Deciding the time wasn't right; I thanked her for her input and said we should talk more later. As if she sensed I had something to ask her, she hesitated before ending the call.

Sixty-One

New Responsibilities

Even though they crossed paths a few times that day, very few words passed between the two dancers. Thinking she upset Chen by mentioning the police, Roxanne went so far as to ask the young Asian woman if she was okay. She ignored the question, and with that, seemingly any bond that had been formed between them.

The blizzard conditions outside the club resulted in the ever-popular pervert's row being almost vacant. A regular, Ronald, sat front and center by himself. He lived in the area and frequently stopped by for the free lunches. The muffin top that hung over his belt was testament to the chicken wings and French fries he ate every day.

Roxanne sat at the bar, making small talk with Rick. Remembering what Norm had asked of her, she tried to think up probing questions. He folded his arms on the bar top and watched Tinkerbell's performance on stage.

"What do you think of her routine, Roxy? Her moves look familiar."

She spun around to face the stage.

"Tinkerbell? Yeah, she's a quick study but a copycat. Her act is a combination of everyone else's."

Rick spoke to her back. "I heard you two have gotten close and you walked her home one-night last week."

"Yeah, she was wasted and there was nobody else left here."

"That's supposed to be Dave's job...he's been fucking up a lot lately and I'm thinking about canning him."

"He's an asshole. I won't miss him."

"How would you feel about taking up some of his slack?"

Roxanne spun back around to face her boss.

"What kind of slack?"

Rick gathered up the paperwork he had spread out on the bar.

"C'mon back to the office. It's easier to talk in there."

She followed him through the lounge and into his office. There was another man sitting behind the desk, looking through a ledger and stack of receipts. Roxanne had seen the man once or twice a week and heard he was a biker. Considering his access to the books, she assumed he was Rick's silent business partner.

"Don't mind Maurice...he's helping me with my taxes."

Rick motioned her to the couch and they both sat down. Roxanne eyed the burly man behind the desk but he carried on as if he didn't exist.

"So, Roxy, are you happy here?"

"Sure. The Asian women have stolen some of my regulars and my tips are down but I do alright."

"They're here to stay. But if you're willing to take on more responsibility, I can throw a little extra cash your way."

Roxanne shifted in her seat, stole another quick glance at Maurice, then turned to her boss.

"What kind of responsibility?"

"I already mentioned Dave, and we're making a few other changes around here...consolidating some jobs you might say. It would mean you'd have to work more hours, are you okay with that? Do you have another job to worry about?"

"I do book keeping for a small chain of sub shops, but I work from home when I'm not here."

Maurice cleared his throat and Roxanne caught him staring, in her peripheral vision. She felt Rick shift his weight on the couch as he leaned back and crossed his legs.

"Really, I didn't know you had *other* talents. Good for you. Listen, I know you've been in the house across the alley, where the chinks live. Nobody is allowed in there...but don't worry, I trust you. As long as you know what happens in there, stays in there."

Roxanne nodded. "For sure. It's none of my business."

"Good answer. My problem is, however, that the woman who ran the house moved on and we need someone to take over some of her responsibilities."

"Like what?"

"The other women seem to look up to you...kinda like a mother figure. No offense. I need someone to keep an eye on them until we can find a replacement for the woman who left."

"I wouldn't have to live there, would I?"

"No, no...nothing like that. They're confined to the house, unless someone escorts them to the doctor's office or for personal shopping. You'd have access to the company van to chauffer them around. I assume you have a valid driver's license?"

Roxanne thought about it, instinctively wondering how she might be able to use the new responsibilities to help the police with their investigation.

"Yes, my license is good. It doesn't sound too difficult; I guess I could try it for a while. When would you want me to start?"

"I'd say today, but nobody should be driving out there in this weather. But maybe you can check the house some-time today and see how their grocery supply is...in case we all get snowed in."

Rick stood up and pulled a ring of keys from his pocket. He removed one and handed it to Roxanne.

"This is for the back door." He grasped her hand. "I'm trusting you with this, Roxy, don't fuck it up. Let's see how you do for a few weeks. If things work out, you never know...maybe you can work on *our* books someday."

He turned to Maurice, who heard the comment, but chose to ignore it.

Sixty-Two

Ice Capades

Chen walked back to the house on her lunch break. A cold gust of wind would have sent her airborne if she hadn't grabbed the fence. Her coat flew open and a whirl of snow wrapped around her like a tornado. With virtually no fat covering her thin frame, the tiny dancer's veins constricted in an attempt to retain her body heat.

Her spiked heels helped with traction, but one caught in the ice on the porch and slipped off her foot. Chen said fuck out loud, it was a word she used often. She repeated the curse three more times when her bare foot landed on the cold ice. With one hand on the door handle for support, she reached down with the other to retrieve her shoe.

Just as her fingers grasped the handle, the door opened, pulling her in with it. Having all her weight on the shoed foot, she lost her balance, fell to the floor, and banged her head on the wall inside. She spewed expletives like water gushing from a firehose, calling the person who opened the door every dirty name she knew.

Flat out on the floor, with a hand behind the sore spot on her head, Chen opened her eyes and saw Roxanne standing over her.

Sixty-Three

Moving Parts

Kevin Bell and I sat down to put our heads together and come up with a plan on how to put Ham into action for The China Syndrome. He said his crew had pinned down the motel primarily used by the women from T & A. The Dew Drop Inn had been a shithole for as long as I'd known it, and rented rooms by the hour. Bell wondered if the motel and bar were somehow connected, or possibly owned by the same criminal organization.

Besides the T & A dancers and some escorts, the only hotel guests were out of town construction workers who paid for rooms weekly. Obviously, one advantage of staying there was that they didn't have to go anywhere else for entertainment. I asked Bell about us renting a room there for surveillance, but he had concerns about being compromised by the management.

I ran an idea by Bell, telling him that Ham was going to visit the strip club and try to take one of the peelers to the motel. My plan was to have him seek out and hook up with Tinkerbell, Roxanne's new friend. If he succeeded in getting her to the room, we would be waiting inside. It could be a great opportunity for us to make contact and gather intelligence.

"That's a lot of moving parts, Norm, and what if she freaks out? Didn't you say the Asian woman was terrified of the police?"

"Yeah, I know...maybe we can figure out a way to get Roxanne there too. I dunno, you're right...too many moving parts."

"Hey, I know things aren't good at home and I've seen your friend naked...you're not tapping that, are you?"

I smiled. "Can't say I haven't thought about it. She's a stripper and a junkie, not a good future there."

"Just wondering...wouldn't want you to get in trouble."

"Says the man on wife number three. Oh yeah...before I forget, Jerry Rice called. Says his immigration searches have come up empty, and he can't really do much for the task force without names or some type of documentation to check out. I see his point; he's wasting his time if the women are being smuggled into the country in shipping containers."

Bell glanced at his watch and scribbled something in his notebook.

"I gotta be somewhere else in twenty minutes. Let me know how it goes with your private dancer."

We parted company and I went back to my desk to check for voicemail. Barney Stoker left a message for me to call him back ASAP. I did and he said he couldn't get ahold of Gamble or Bell so he left us all messages. Being the first to respond, the Mountie told me he got stonewalled by their Montreal office when he reached out.

Thinking his counterparts had purposely put him off, Stoker checked with one of his new cronies in CSIS. He told me the intelligence service was involved in a joint investigation with the RCMP Internal Affairs, looking into corruption in the Montreal Police, and a possible connection to one of their own, in Commercial Crime.

His source wouldn't elaborate about the investigation on the phone but disclosed that it had something to do with one of the Chinese Triads and the shipping port. Barney told me he was on the way up the 401 when he called, that he was going to poke around personally. He added that he'd check back in after he got there. His hands-on approach impressed me. Maybe I had underestimated the man.

Sixty-Four

No Onions

Roxanne caught me on the way out to grab a bite for lunch. I was still on the low carb kick and was in the Burger King drive through when she called. Telling her to hang on a minute, I ordered a double beef Whopper with cheese, heavy mayo and no onions. My mouth salivated while placing the order. Juggling the phone and my wallet while trying to drive, I told Roxanne I'd call her back shortly.

I asked for extra napkins when I picked up my burger. Experience taught me there'd be a big mess when I scraped all the good stuff off the bun and discarded the bread. Finding the nearest empty parking spot, I went to work in my lap. Food first...being a man who got grumpy when hungry, Roxanne would have to wait her turn.

I tasted raw onion on my first bite, and was pissed off for not seeing it buried in the extra mayonnaise. Glancing over at the line up in the drive through, I decided it wasn't worth the effort to return my meal. I'd worry about the onion-breath later. An image of a nude Roxanne on stage, stuck in my mind while I inhaled my tasteless burger. They were so much better when they first came out, before they took to nuking them.

Roxanne called me back before her dance left my head. I took a hit of diet cola and answered the phone.

"Well, did you get it your way?"

Momentarily confused, my dirty mind was stuck on her naked image.

"Your Whopper...their slogan?"

"Oh, yeah...I mean no, they fucked up my order, as usual. Anyway, what's up girl?"

"You won't believe it, Storm, I did like you said and got closer to Rick...he gave me a key to the house and wants me to drive the Asians around, and I saw this guy...Maurice, I think he's Rick's silent partner. I..."

"Holy shit...slow down...are you on speed?"

"Sorry, I've got so much to tell you...where are you now?"

"Downtown."

"Me too...I just dropped off the books at the sub shop on Ouellette. Can we meet somewhere?"

"Sure...how about the riverfront...down by the train, in the parking lot?"

"Okay, see ya there, Copper."

Sixty-Five

Next?

I met with Roxanne and filled two full pages in my journal with notes. I'd never seen her so pumped and excited. She acted more like a crackhead, than an opiate junkie. As I watched and listened to her, I had to wonder if she was weaning herself off the stuff. Being a police agent, and having a new purpose, definitely looked good on her.

She seemed high on life, and we continued to talk about other things after she filled me in on what was happening at the club. Roxanne said she hoped to buy another car with the extra cash. I glanced over at her aged and rusted Toyota, nodding in agreement. With her book keeping job and new responsibilities at the strip bar, she thought she might even be able to give up taking her clothes off for a living.

Her upbeat and positive attitude made me look at her in a different light. She couldn't dance forever, and there had to be an afterlife for someone like her. I knew where my mind was heading so I told her I had to get back to work. Roxanne thanked me and squeezed my arm before leaving the car. I admired her shape in tight jeans, when she walked away.

When I got back to the office, the last of my crew were on the way out the door. Gelinas said Gamble was already gone so the five-after rule was in effect. That meant everyone bailed five minutes after the boss left. I dumped my portable radio in the charger and dropped the car keys while trying to hang them up.

My back groaned when I scooped them off the floor. Snow flurries outside the window caught my eye. Shuffling over for a better look, I admired the partial view of the Detroit skyline. The city looked so peaceful from our side of the river. Massaging my lower back with my palms, I thought about Roxanne and the woman she called China Doll.

Deciding to head home like everyone else, I closed up shop and made my way to the parking garage. Being on autopilot, my busy brain got me home without remembering the drive there. Thinking about the strip club, the Asian dancers and their STD's, Roxanne became the common denominator in the formulation of a plan that started coming together in my head.

Sixty-Six

Uncle Ben

Chen did her best to avoid Roxanne, but in all honesty, she missed talking to her only friend. If anyone could track down Big Mike or help her escape, it would be Roxanne. She seemed to be purposely getting in Chen's way, trying to get her attention.

Having her mentor coming into the house made it even more difficult to avoid her. When Roxanne cornered her in the kitchen and asked what she wanted from the grocery store, Chen couldn't stand the silence between them anymore. She threw herself at Roxanne and hugged her like a long-lost sister.

Two other women made food requests but Roxanne ignored them. The two friends were on their own channel, in their own little world. They shared apologies and shed tears. Roxanne handed her pen and paper to one of the other dancers and told her to list whatever they needed. She was busy catching up with her friend. After the other women wrote out their wish list and left the room, Roxanne asked Chen if she wanted to go shopping with her.

She was reluctant at first, saying their house matron was the only one who took them outside the house, but nobody knew when she was coming back. Roxanne smiled and explained she was her replacement, temporarily, and Rick said she was to look after their needs, and do things like taking them to the doctor.

Glancing around the room to make sure they were alone, Roxanne said she was in charge now and didn't see why Chen couldn't accompany her grocery shopping. The two women hit the road and never stopped talking until they were inside the store. The China Doll stopped in the middle of the rice isle, and stood slack-jawed.

"I've never seen so many different brands of rice and such a huge store...everything you need is here." She laughed at the picture of Uncle Ben on one bag. "Who is this man...he doesn't look Chinese?"

Roxanne looked at the man's portrait for the first time in her life.

"Somebody's rich uncle, for sure."

They stopped at the pharmacy to pick up a handful of prescriptions for the Asian women and Roxanne recognized the name of a certain drug in Chen's medication.

"There's one here for you...are you sick?"

"It's for steeds...many of the others have the same thing."

"What the fuck is steeds?"

"From sex with men."

"Oh, you mean STD's...sexually transmitted diseases...don't you use protection?"

"Yes, but some men like going bareback and pay more for it. I first got sick in China, but caught more diseases since then. I get shots and take pills."

"Oh hon...this scrip is for hepatitis...that's bad."

"The doctor says we'll all be fine as long as we take our medication."

"I don't think he's giving you the whole story. What's his name?"

"Dr. Yin, at the clinic...we all go to the same man...you will see when you drive us there for our check-ups and medication."

While driving back to the house, Roxanne decided she had to hook her friend up with Norm Strom. Maybe she could swing it during a visit to the doctor's office and the cops could find out more about the quack. She saw Chen staring out the window at the Ambassador Bridge, looming in the distance.

"Where does that go?"

"The bridge? It goes to Detroit and the United States."

"You mean America?"

Roxanne made a right turn and headed north.

"Yeah, you've never seen the riverfront here?"

"We see nothing, only the inside of this van and the doctor's office. Other times they move us in vans or trucks with no windows so we never know where we're going."

Pulling into one of the riverfront parks, Roxanne pointed to Detroit.

"That's America, on the other side of the river."

Chen's mouth hung open and she stared in awe.

"It's so close...is it far to California?"

Roxanne scoffed. "About three thousand miles...why?"

"Just wondering...when I was first taken, one of the other girls always said she wanted to go there and be a movie star. The river reminds me of Shanghai...where my mother took me on the big Ferris wheel."

She let the van idle while Chen took in the panorama, and committed a list of things to memory she wanted to tell Norm. The cops had to help the Asian women. They were treated as nothing more than sex slaves.

Pulling out of the parking lot, Roxanne let it slip she really wanted Chen to meet her friend, the police officer. Before her friend could object, she added he was a good man and dedicated cop. He could not only help her reach her doorman friend in Montreal, but maybe help locate her family back home. The last part was a stretch, and she knew it as soon as the words left her lips, but the expression on Chen's face said it all.

"He can do that...find my family?"

Roxanne tightened her jaw, trying not to frown. There was no backtracking now.

"He's helped me in the past, and I completely trust him. The police in Canada are a lot different than where you come from. There might be a few bad apples, but they're all connected by computers and phones now, and they track down people all over the world. All you have to do is meet with him and decide for yourself...I'll be there with you."

Chen, deep in thought, stared out the window. Worry-lines at the corners of her eyes confirmed she wasn't a young girl anymore.

"Okay, I'll talk to him."

Sixty-Seven

Christmas Trees

Sleep wasn't a problem for me. Whether it was my marital bullshit or work-related stuff stimulating neural circuits in my brain, I was able to find the off-switch, and saw logs until the alarm clock went off...most of the time. Waking before the morning music, my thoughts picked up where they left off when I passed out.

Not being a morning person, I found it odd how the quiet and empty house rattled me a bit. It was loneliness. Having come from a large family, moving in with a buddy, and then getting married, I'd never really spent much time living by myself. I enjoyed my alone time, but missed being with someone...weird.

The long drive to work became routine. It was the perfect time to plan the day ahead. The scenery was always the same, and my mind more occupied with work, than the road in front of me. I got in early and was the first one in the office. Peace and quiet, I could get so much more work done if it was always like that.

Working the China Syndrome task force meant I gave up my night shift, and it got me out of doing the morning paperwork. One of the other Detectives and his crew were responsible for that now. Before they came in and I got in their way, I checked for any phone and email messages.

With my journal in hand, I headed across the hall to the project room. The door was unlocked when I grabbed the handle and I was surprised to see Barney Stoker. He was busy putting the syndicate's organizational chart up on the white board, but managed a 'morning' without turning around. I returned the greeting and sat down to see what he was doing.

Written in green marker, it reminded me of a Christmas tree, with a question mark on top where the star would sit. Stoker had listed names, numbered companies, businesses, and their cities or countries. There weren't many ornaments on his tree. Mostly question marks dangled from the branches. He did a lot of work in a short time, but we had a long way to go before we could light up our tree.

Watching the big man work, I imagined him being the poster boy for the RCMP. He reminded me of the cartoon character, Dudley Do-Right. Stoker was in good shape for his age. My guess...it was more the result of good genetics than a proper diet and workout regimen.

Following his chart from top to bottom, I recognized the flow of human trafficking my new CI friend laid out. Her real name was Chen Shen. We needed a lot more information from her. I skimmed my notes from the meet with Roxanne, and stepped up to the next white board to start my own chart.

The Mountie stopped at Montreal so that's where I started. From there I drew lines to Kingston, Niagara Falls, and Windsor. I added the names of clubs, owners, and associates I was aware of. Using stage names protected the identities of our agent and the Asian dancer.

We had another team meeting scheduled that morning. Even though it wasn't to start for another hour, Bell and our Intelligence guy came in, quietly took seat, and checked out our work. A few minutes later, Jones from Intelligence stepped up beside me and asked if he could add something. From Montreal, he added branches to London and Sarnia, with strip clubs named in each city.

The four of us were openly discussing the organizational charts when Gamble and the Inspector poked their heads into the room. The latter motioned for us to carry on, while he and my boss looked over the white boards. Bell used a pause in our conversation to ask the two men if they needed anything. My Inspector apologized for the interruption and said he was looking for an update to bring to the morning meeting in the Chief's office. He told us to keep up the good work.

The rest of the team trickled in ahead of the scheduled start time. Obviously, everyone was eager to get something done. While the group took in the posted information and discussed it among themselves, I called over to my office to have our co-op student make a coffee run. One of the Constables told me the Inspector already took care of it.

The morning goodies arrived while I was hanging up the phone. Once everyone had a wake-up in hand, I rolled my chair up to Carrie Smith and ran an idea by her I'd been kicking around in my head. We stopped talking when Stoker asked for everyone's attention. He said he wanted to bring us up to speed on his trip to Montreal.

The RCMP Corporal with the new CSIS credentials, reported mixed results during his fact-finding mission. Referring to his organizational chart, he was able to confirm that a Chinese Triad with roots in Shanghai and Hong Kong, was running a huge smuggling operation. They had connections in shipping and various international ports, allowing them to move contraband around the world.

According to him, the Mounties, Interpol, and other police agencies across the globe had open investigations into that particular triad for the past three years. The RCMP and Montreal Police were currently looking into the Canadian end of their operation. His boss at CSIS told him he couldn't elaborate on corruption within the Montreal PD, but confirmed an active investigation involving Montreal Police.

Kevin Bell and I exchanged glances. We both knew if CSIS and the RCMP had their way, our investigation would drag on for months, if not years. There were too many levels of the syndicate to uncover in too many countries, with too many players involved. From experience, the Morality Sergeant and I knew federal investigations always set their sights on the big fish. We weren't fishing in the same pond.

I passed Carrie a note, offering to buy her lunch if she stuck around after the meeting. She smiled and nodded. I was hungry, in more ways than one, and my friend looked good enough to eat. Gamble called the meeting about twenty minutes later, when Stoker ran out of steam. We all went our separate ways and Carrie followed me to my office.

Bell and Gamble stood in his office doorway when my friend and I walked into Street Crimes. I asked if the four of us could have a private conversation. My boss let us in and closed the door. He got comfortable behind his desk and scanned the three faces opposite him.

"It's nice to see the Mounties are digging into this, but Stoker had more question marks on that board than the Riddler had on his costume. We can't wait for them...do you guys have a better plan or quicker solution?"

Bell turned to me. "Norm?"

"Carrie and I talked about health regulations, privacy laws, and the deplorable conditions in the house where the Asian women are living."

My Staff Sergeant appeared puzzled. "Go on..."

"Here's my thinking. We've got surveillance from the Morality Unit verifying ongoing prostitution inside the strip club and at the Dew Drop Inn, along with corroborating testimony from our agent on that and the conditions inside the bawdy house. Carrie has health records that show a dangerous outbreak of STDs among the Asian women who are all living in that same house.

They all go to the same clinic and are examined by the same doctor." I glanced at Carrie. "And correct me if I'm wrong, we believe these women to be illegal, yet they are somehow getting expensive prescription medications for different ailments. I agree we can't wait for everyone else to catch up. We need to act now."

Bell nodded along in silence. Gamble's gaze rested on his twiddling thumbs in front of him, on the desk. He sighed, and eyed Bell. "Kevin?"

"I agree. From what I'm hearing, we could try a general warrant to search the house. The clinic could prove more difficult, but with Carrie's office on board, I think we have a good shot."

Gamble digested Bell's comments for a moment, then puffed his cheeks and blew air. "Fuck it...let's do it. What do they say...it's better to ask forgiveness than permission?

Let's keep this between us until we have warrants ready to go. Then we'll see if the others want in. It will be too late then, for them to say no."

Bell said he'd get into it, meaning the warrant applications.

I asked Carrie to give me a second to grab my coat. My wife and her co-worker came in the side door as we exited. The awkward silence and odd looks could have made for a good story.

Sixty-Eight

Eavesdropping

Business was slow. Roxanne thought up excuses to get out of the club and maybe enjoy the sunshine outside. Winter was upon the city, and sunny days were rare. She was still in her street clothes and decided to take the company van out for gas and a wash. Getting to the closed office door, she heard loud voices inside.

Roxanne had seen Maurice exiting his car when she arrived at work, and assumed he was in the office with Rick. Trying to block out the club's music, she plugged one ear and put the other to the door. It was the two owners arguing about the Asian dancers. Rick said they were making good money for the club but his silent partner said they were nothing but diseased whores.

There were comments about the latest results from the doctor and it might be time to bring in some new talent. Maurice rambled off some of the women's names but the door muffled his voice and she couldn't tell if he mentioned Tinkerbell. Rick urged him to wait for test results on the other half of the dancers before sending any of them away.

His partner brought up the embarrassing complaints from important clients.

Roxanne changed positions to hear better but the office door suddenly swung open. She lost her footing and re-actively reached out for it. "Oh...sorry, I was just about to knock. Is Rick in there?"

Maurice stormed past her.

Her boss's voice shouted from inside the office. "What is it?"

Roxanne slithered into the room. "Um...I was coming to get the van keys and gas it up...didn't notice until I parked it the tank was empty. It could use a wash too."

He gestured toward the hooks on the wall.

She quickly snatched the keys and turned to leave.

"What were you doing out there?"

Fuck... how does he know I was listening...is there a camera outside the door? "Nothing...it's really slow and like I said, the van needs gas."

"That's not what I'm talking about."

Roxanne froze and didn't know what to say next. Only imagining his reaction, she started to tremble.

"When you went for groceries the other day...you took one of the Chinks with you. I thought you knew bet-ter...they're not to leave the house unless they're working or going to the clinic. Speaking of which...six more need to go right away. Make it happen."

Roxanne exhaled the breath she'd been holding and stepped toward the desk to retrieve the note in Rick's hand.

"Here's the list of names."

She took the paper and turned to leave.

"Hang on a second." He retrieved an envelope from his desk drawer and handed it to her. "It's for the doctor at the clinic, Yin. Make an appointment for yourself and give this to him when you're behind closed doors. Can you handle that?"

Roxanne noticed her hand was shaking when she took the envelope. "Sure, Rick, I'll take care of it."

By the time she got to the locker room and grabbed her coat, Roxanne was vibrating. Worried she might bump into Maurice again she hurried from the club and climbed into the van. Fighting the urge to get high, she grabbed a pack of cigarettes from her purse instead. She took a couple deep breaths and tried to steady her hands to light up. Filling her lungs, she held the smoke to let the nicotine work its magic.

She found Chen's name on Rick's list. What did it all mean? Were they going to get rid of the women they had and bring in new ones? What would happen to Chen? Different scenarios ran through her mind. Roxanne reached for the gearshift, but stopped short and took out her phone instead. She had to call Norm.

While listening to the ringtone someone banged on her window and scared the shit out of her. It was Maurice. She immediately felt sick to her stomach. The glass was foggy and he put his face within an inch of it, staring at her. Roxanne felt as if she was frozen in time, in a bad nightmare and she couldn't wake up. He knocked again and motioned for her to roll the window down. She complied.

"Hey, Rick says you're going for gas...can you grab me a couple packs of smokes?"

"S-sure...what kind?"

"Export A's, large. And can I mooch a couple of yours until you get back? Fuck...it's freezing out here...I thought Windsor was supposed to be in the banana belt."

Roxanne handed Maurice three cigarettes. He said thanks, closed the collar on his coat, and walked away. Remembering the phone fell in her lap, she reached between her legs and checked to see if she peed herself.

Sixty-Nine

Lunch Date

Carrie Smith and I went to the Penalty Box for lunch and both ordered their Chicken Delight. We talked about our party days when I was in patrol and she handed out parking tickets. My platoon included a great group of guys that year. Sadly, we all moved on to different job placements. I confessed to having a crush on her since the night we met. I waited for a response.

My friend blushed, and sipped from the straw in her cola. I took her by surprise. I don't think she knew what to say. My drink was near empty and the waitress dropped off a refill before I could ask her for one. It appeared Carrie was about to respond to my comment, when my phone rang. Roxanne's number showed on the call display.

Carrie smiled. "Saved by the bell."

"Sorry, I have to get this...it's my informant from our project."

With no immediate need for privacy, I answered the call from our table.

"Storm, we gotta talk...where are you?"

"I'm having lunch with a friend. What's up?"

"I need to see you...all hell's breaking loose. Can you meet me, now?"

With my eyes still on Carrie, I shrugged and raised my brow. "Shortly...where?"

"On the west side...how about behind the Bowlero?"

"Give me ten...see you there."

Carrie had already signaled for our check. "Duty calls, eh? Will you have time to drop me off downtown where I left my car?"

"Are you in any hurry to get back to work?"

"Not really, my boss knows I had a meeting with the task force."

"All right...how about you tag along and meet a real live informant?" I threw enough cash down to cover lunch. We grabbed our coats and headed for the door.

"Do you think it'll be all right...will she mind?"

"I don't know...probably not. She's pretty cool for a stripper with a drug habit."

Carrie's eyes grew big, as if I just told her I was really a woman.

Roxanne was hard to miss, sitting in the company van with the life-size image of a scantily clad exotic dancer displayed on the side. I pulled up to the driver's side and suggested she jump in my car, since her vehicle stuck out in the empty bowling alley lot. She got in the back seat and I made the introductions while she checked out Carrie.

"She's a lot cuter than your last partner, Storm."

"Carrie's not a cop. She works for the Board of Health."

"Yeah? That's one of the things I have to tell you about..."

The next ten minutes were a blur. I scribbled notes in my journal as fast as I could, trying to keep up. Stealing a quick glance at Carrie, I saw she was completely mesmerized. Roxanne fumbled in her purse for her cigarettes. Smoking was something I never allowed in my car, but she was shaking so bad I told her to roll down her window and blow the smoke outside.

"Shit, I almost forgot." Roxanne pulled out the envelope Rick gave her. "This is for the doctor at the clinic...I didn't open it but can tell it's full of cash."

Carrie touched my hand. It was on the armrest between us. "Can I say something, Norm?"

"Sure, go ahead."

"I know we already discussed this in your office earlier, but after listening to Roxanne I sense more of a need for urgency. Infectious diseases are a serious threat and these women need to be either quarantined or taken out of circulation. We also need to look into the doctor. My boss is going to freak out when I bring him up to speed."

Roxanne flicked her half-finished cigarette out the window.

"Sorry, but your friend's right, Storm, you gotta do something soon. If they ship this group of women out, who knows what the club will do next?"

Carrie seemed to be searching for something to say to my CI. "You're a brave woman, Roxanne. I just want to say we all appreciate what you're doing. It could save lives."

I considered what I heard and what our next play should be. I let the two women chat while I called Kevin Bell.

"Hey, how's it going with the search warrants?"

Seventy

Once Upon a Time

It would have been great to have Roxanne wired up for her conversation with the doctor at the clinic, but with the speed things were progressing, there wasn't time. I hoped to meet Chen too, but we had enough information to obtain our warrants, and she could fill in the blanks later, after we executed the searches and brought everyone in.

There wasn't time to photocopy the doctor's money either, I held up Roxanne long enough and she had to get back before they missed her. We did have time, however, to open and examine the money in the envelope and mark some of the bills. Carrie popped into the bowling alley and borrowed a replacement for one we damaged.

Back at the office, I brought my boss up to speed. Across the hall, in the project room, I repeated the update to Bell. He was busy writing his application for the search warrants. Taking to the laptop across the table, I began typing the pertinent information he would need. With the convenience of electronic word processing, Bell would only need to cut and paste my report into his. Filling out the 'Information to Obtain a Search Warrant' was like telling a short story, with a plot and cast of characters.

I'd written over a hundred of them, most while in narcotics, and was tempted on more than one occasion, to start my request with, 'once upon a time'. However, search warrants were serious business; documents would be read by the judiciary upon application, and later scrutinized by Crown and defense counsels. Bell and I got lost in our work.

Gamble popped his head in the room at one point and said he left the office door open and the day shift had checked out.

"I don't care if you guys want to stay, but you can always finish up tomorrow."

The Taz was in the zone and didn't even look up.

I spun my chair around to face my boss.

"We're gonna take it as far as we can tonight...my CI is supposed to get back to me later, after she takes the peelers to the clinic. I'll add that info tomorrow. Kevin will work out our operational plan for the raids, while we wait for the warrants. We should be ready to hit our targets Wednesday morning, nice and early, while everyone is still in bed."

Seventy-One

The Doctor

Roxanne rounded up the dancers on the list. Tinkerbell was one of them. She pulled her aside and told her to keep their chat cordial...they could trust no one. Chen asked if, and when she would be meeting the policeman. She was anxious to find Big Mike and get her money. Roxanne told her friend she would fill her in later.

Doing as Rick directed her to, Roxanne made a doctor's appointment for herself, along with the other women. Waiting in the lobby was nerve-racking, and she wished she could light up a smoke. Sitting on her hands in case someone noticed them shaking, Roxanne was surprised when they called her name first. The receptionist showed her to an examination room.

The five-minute wait seemed like an hour. An Asian doctor came in and introduced himself. There was no hesitation on his part. Yin said he knew she was coming and asked if she had something for him. Roxanne removed the envelope from her purse and handed it to the doctor. He fingered the thickness of the package, held it up to the light, and stuffed it into an inside pocket of his lab coat. Doctor

Yin told her to wait a few minutes before leaving, as if she had to put her clothes back on.

When she returned to the waiting room, one of the other women went in. It didn't register at first, but Roxanne heard the receptionist use the woman's real name. With the exception of Chen, she only knew them by their stage names.

Sitting down and thinking about it, sadness suddenly overwhelmed her. Every one of the Asian women probably had a similar story. For the first time, Roxanne saw them as victims. Scanning their hardened faces and distant stares, she wanted to cry. They were all human, just like her. She took a deep breath to control her emotions.

A warm sensation grew in her stomach. She thought about how her reporting to the police might help the women. It instilled in her a sense of pride. Getting justice for them was the least she could do, and probably the most descent thing she ever did in her life. She took in the other women again. It was as if they were caged animals waiting for her to set them free.

Seventy-Two

Team Players

Staff Sergeant Gamble, Sergeant Bell, Carrie Smith, and myself, met for breakfast on Tuesday to strategize for the task force meeting later in the morning. We wanted to make sure we had all the right answers to the hard questions from Corporal Stoker. He was sure to ask why we were taking action so early in our investigation.

He and all the others involved in our project, were invited to the raids in the spirit of cooperation. It was a team effort, and we hoped to boost the RCMP investigation with any pertinent information we recovered. We had our reasons for the early attack on the bottom level of the crime syndicate. It would take some convincing for the others, who in turn, had to explain our actions to people higher up on the totem pole.

The project room filled with the same faces I saw at our first meeting on The China Syndrome. Bell and I did some tidying prior to the meeting...stuffing accumulated information into the files and boxes sitting on cabinets along the back wall. The two organizational charts were condensed, printed, and put on the front page of the operational packages placed in front of each person.

The white boards now showed the different target locations and the team members who would execute the searches at each one. The raids were to occur simultaneously on Wednesday morning at 9am, as listed on the warrants. We completed separate arrest warrants for Rick Thompson, Maurice Levesque, and Doctor Wang Yong Yin.

After letting everyone settle in and browse their op packages, Gamble addressed the room. My Staff Sergeant focused on Stoker when he told everyone we decided to take early action in the interest of public safety. Before the Mountie could interject, Gamble said the triad was planning to move the Asian women again, and we could easily lose our inside source.

I watched Stoker's reaction. He sucked in his lower lip and bit down on it. It was obvious he had an opinion but he kept it to himself. I was sure he knew we were doing the right thing, and his people in Montreal could use whatever we gleaned from our investigation to bolster theirs. He sat back in his chair and bobbed his head just enough to tell me he was on board.

The discussion following Gamble's briefing was all positive, with mostly questions about communications and logistics. We agreed that anyone arrested went to Windsor Police Headquarters and the Asian women to a holding room, down the street at the Immigration office. Officials would interview them there. We thought it important they felt safe and they were not under arrest.

Exhausted when I got home that evening, the leftover pizza casserole in the fridge proved to be my perfect remedy. A concoction constructed in my crockpot; I included all my favorite pizza toppings minus the noodles. It was only 8pm, but I felt ready for bed. My thoughts about having a second helping were interrupted by a phone call from one of my sisters. My father suffered a heart attack and was in the hospital.

Luckily, there were no radar traps on my way back into the city. The thirty-five-minute trip seemed like ten. My siblings, stepmother, stepsisters, and accompanying spouses, were all in the waiting room. The middle sister was on the phone with the youngest, who resided in Vancouver.

The news wasn't good...a myocardial infarction from coronary thrombosis...or something to that effect. After some waiting and updates from nurses, and finally the doctor, my stepmother told us dad was stabilized and would undergo bypass surgery the next day. We shared hugs and shed a few tears together.

I absorbed the grief around me and examined my own feelings. I cried at the end of Green Beret, a John Wayne flick, and wondered why a family tragedy didn't affect me the same way. It seemed strange, but I was the same way at funerals.

In fact, the last good cry I had was while discussing my marital woes with my estranged wife. Other than that, I couldn't remember the last time. Being the big brother, I hung around. The others slowly retreated from the hospital waiting room and made their way home. Eventually, I left two of my steps with their mother, and headed out myself.

Just outside the city limits, my phone rang. Of course, I feared the worst. It was only Roxanne checking in. Already wondering if I could stay awake for the ride home, her conversation was a welcome diversion. She filled me in earlier in the day about the visit to the doctor's office, and called to see what would happen in the morning when we conducted our raids.

In my opinion, she asked silly questions. I addressed her concerns and assured her we knew what we were doing, and it wasn't my first rodeo. Roxanne joked about me being a cowboy, and wondered about taking me for a ride. I welcomed the sexual teasing, unsure if she was serious. It had been a while and just the thought of sex aroused me.

We chatted for my entire ride home. It wasn't until I pulled into my driveway and glanced at the clock that I realized how late it was. I needed sleep. We ended our call and I shuffled into the house. I set the alarm for 6am and swore only twenty minutes had passed when it went off and woke me up.

Seventy-Three

Raid!

It's funny, the things you think about in the heat of the moment. A silly picture formed in my mind when Kevin Bell gave the order for all the raids to commence. It was the stupid commercial for Raid; the one where all the cockroaches scatter before being sprayed with bug killer.

Fortunately, most everyone was sleeping and they didn't have a chance to evade the teams of cops and other government officials. Only one location got a bit chaotic, the bawdy house where all the Asian women lived. Strange men in uniform, some carrying guns, freaked out more than one of the dancers.

They hid in closets, tried to run for doors, and one attempted to climb out an upstairs window. The quick reactions of Constable King probably saved the woman from serious injury. He caught her arm on the way out. Oddly enough, one of the dancers sat quietly on her mattress, with a packed bag beside her.

Someone called me upstairs to the bedroom, thinking the woman was planning to escape. Our eyes met and something seemed familiar. She was a bit slimmer than the others and, in my opinion, a lot prettier.

Her gaze went right through me. I compared it to the fifty-yard stare of some soldiers after being in combat. I wasn't sure, but thought the corners of her flattened lips tried to form a smile. It was her...I knew it right then and there. Careful not to give her away, I waited until the other women left the room.

"Chen Shen?"

Her eyes grew wide and glazed over. She nodded once, dropped her shoulders, and let all the air escape from her lungs. I put out a hand to help her up.

"I'm Norm Strom...Roxanne's friend. It's all over now...you're safe. And I'm sorry, but you'll have to go with the other women...to make it look good. Don't worry, I'll hook up with you later, and we can talk about what will happen next."

Her wounded look reminded me of a puppy being scolded for peeing on the carpet. She gripped my hand and didn't let go until we stepped into the hallway.

"Roxanne?"

"She's fine. I'm not sure how or when, but I'll try to get you together with her later. Everything will be alright...just be honest and answer any questions you might be asked."

"You're not staying with me?"

I felt like I was leaving that same puppy home alone for the first time.

"I can't right now...we're trying to find Rick and Maurice...to arrest them."

Chen smiled as she climbed into the van with the other women.

I went back into the house to find Carrie Smith. She stood in the middle of the kitchen, taking notes.

"Did you find the woman you were looking for?"

"I did...just put her in the van with the others."

"I can't believe the living conditions in here...twelve women sharing dirty mattresses and only one bathroom..."

A small cockroach fell from the ceiling and landed in Carrie's hair, near her shoulder. I reached out and quickly flicked it away.

"What the hell was that?"

"A housefly." I didn't have the heart to tell her.

She tossed her golden locks from side to side, and instinctively shook her shoulders.

"This place is disgusting...I saw cockroaches when I opened the cupboard under the sink. I'm getting the willies, are we done in here?"

"I am. You can wait in my car if you like, while I go check on Bell."

She happily accepted the keys and quick-walked to the door. I strolled across the alley to the T & A Gentlemen's Club where Bell was almost finished ransacking the office. Surveying the mess, I casually glanced his way.

Bell shook his head. "We've got the books—not the real ones of course so we're checking for hidden compartments."

"Maybe Rick or Maurice has the other copy with them."

"Not at Rick's...they arrested him, but haven't found anything useful there. Have you heard anything from team Maurice?"

"No, but how hard can it be to search a motel room? I'll look into it...don't want to disturb any of your mess in here."

"You get the girl?"

"Yep...she was packed and ready to go. I'm sure she's happy it's all over."

"Yeah, maybe...now those women have to deal with health and immigration officials. But you're right, they've gotta be headed to a better place."

I went outside to join Carrie in my car, and phoned Stoker at Maurice's motel.

"He's in the wind, Norm. Manager says he pays by the month but only stays two or three nights a week. The shower stall is still wet...my guess is he left before we got here and headed back to Montreal. I already put a call in to my people on that end. How'd you guys make out?"

"All the Asian women are accounted for and Bell has the doctored books, but Maurice probably has the one's we want. We really need those if we're going to connect the triad to the operation here."

Stoker sighed, grunted something in response, and ended the call. I headed for my car.

As if waiting her turn, Roxanne's number popped up on my screen before the phone had a chance to ring. It was barely after ten in the morning, but she sounded like she was five coffees into her day.

"Storm, what's going on...how'd you make out...is Chen alright?"

"Uh...lots, pretty good, and Chen is fine. We're still sorting things out and looking for one of the owners."

"Who, Rick?"

"No, Maurice...he's MIA."

"Huh, what's that mean? Did you get Rick...find any drugs in the office? I've seen him doing coke in there. When can I see Chen?"

I couldn't help myself and laughed. Bell's nickname was Taz, but Roxanne was wound tighter than a tornado.

"Easy, girl, get some food into your stomach. You sound like you're on crack. Give me a couple hours to see how things play out and I'll get back to you when I know more. Chen's going to be busy with Health and Immigration people for a while. Don't worry about her, I've got it."

I noticed Carrie was staring at me when I put away my phone. "Anyone ever tell you; you have a great profile?"

"What?"

"Nothing...I was just listening in...so many moving parts to this thing. A lot more excitement than I've ever seen in one morning. Any report from the Doctor's office yet?"

"That's Shorty's team...he had the simple task of seizing a few files and arresting the doctor if he was there. But height isn't the only area he's challenged in."

Carrie chuckled, but probably didn't know what I meant. She gazed out the passenger window while I headed downtown. Using the lull in the action, I dialed my sister to see how dad was doing. According to her, they did a double bypass and repaired one valve. Things apparently went well and he was in recovery. Ending the call, I saw Carrie was staring at me again.

Her mouth was agape. "Your father had heart surgery?"

"Yeah, but it sounds like he'll be fine."

"Jesus Christ, Norm, didn't you just tell me a few weeks ago that your mother's cancer is back?"

"Yep...I'm supposed to bring her in for treatment tomorrow afternoon...same hospital my dad's in. Guess I can visit him while she's busy getting radiation."

"And you're working today...shouldn't you..."

"I'm good. Like I said, I'll see mom tomorrow and check in on dad. It'll save me on parking."

Carrie shook her head, then reached over and placed her hand on my arm.

"My God, Norm, you're recently separated too...I don't know how you handle it all."

I shrugged.

"Lots of family for support, and my mom just lives down the street from me."

She squeezed my forearm before letting go. I knew better than to make eye contact right then because we were both vulnerable, and I might want to pull off the road somewhere to jump her bones. I tried to hide a smile, thinking to myself how sex could solve all my problems.

Seventy-Four

Dirty Laundry

Knowing there were hours of paperwork and interviews ahead of me, I debated on whether or not to pick up something to eat. It was hard to follow my diet when I was busy and out on the road. It was as if the food gods answered my prayers when I saw trays of munchies being carried through the front doors of the station.

Pangs of hunger quickened my step. I parked in the garage, headed up the elevator, and paused in the project room doorway. The buzz of activity filled the room. Worried the food I saw wasn't for us, I regretted not stopping earlier.

Gamble stood on the opposite side of the hallway. I heard shouting coming from inside our office.

"Hey boss, what's that all about?"

"Stoker is in my office...with the door closed. It sounds like he was on the losing end of a heated discussion, but I think he's gaining ground now. Any problems with your raids?"

"I'm hungry...saw some food being delivered..."

"Don't worry, Norm, it's on the way up—meat and cheese and veggie trays, just for you."

I smiled. "All good at the house. I found Chen and she seemed okay. I heard Bell couldn't find the books we want. They might be with Maurice, who's in the wind."

"I heard. Kevin just called me...he found a floor safe hidden under the carpet, below the desk. We're bringing Rick back there to open it. He decided to cooperate when Bell told him the warrant allowed us to take a jackhammer to it."

"Anything from Shorty and the good Doctor?"

"Good move putting Gelinas on his team. She found more files than there are women...seems Yin had his own scam going, getting government kickbacks on fake clients. She also found the envelope of cash with your marked bills in his desk drawer. I think it's safe to say he's fucked."

Stoker came out of Gamble's office and left the door open.

"Sorry, it got a bit loud in there. Bell is on the horn for you."

My boss went to answer his phone. Stoker leaned on the file cabinet beside me and blew air from his puffed cheeks.

"Tough day in the trenches?"

"My boss...said he would've appreciated a heads up on the raids before now. When I mentioned dirty cops and the usual leaks, he hit the roof. He calmed down some when I told him what we've accomplished so far. I do sympathize with him...CSIS is still fairly new and trying to prove itself in the intelligence world."

"Yeah, well, after today you'll have boxes of fresh intel he can sift through. Any more word on Maurice?"

"No, but my guys are sitting on his apartment and his clubs in Montreal. If he surfaces in any of those locations, we'll nab him. I can only hope he has the books...I'll be getting another earful if we strike out."

Gamble called Stoker and I into his office.

"Bell got into the safe. No books...but a good chunk of cash, some cocaine, and a bundle of documents for the Asian women...a few passports and other government ID's, maybe fake. He says the papers look legit, but it's all Chinese to him."

I laughed, but Stoker didn't get the joke. Maybe he was shell-shocked, after his boss blasted him. King walked by Gamble's doorway carrying food. That was my cue.

After filling my stomach with food, and my ears with positive news of evidence collected during our raids, I drove over to the Immigration office. It was only a few blocks away. I waited in the lobby for at least fifteen minutes, before my task force liaison finally showed up.

I felt she was stonewalling me, but I trusted Officer Gingras from the time we worked together in narcotics. In fairness to her, I sensed pressure from above. The bottom line...the women were illegal aliens, and Canadian officials were attempting to negotiate with their Chinese counterparts.

Carrie Smith appeared from another office, off the lobby, and took the empty seat beside me. Gingras nodded and walked away.

"What the fuck's going on, girl?"

"What you'd expect...a battle of bosses...mine against Immigration and the Canadian and Chinese Consulates."

"I was really hoping to talk to Chen. What do you think is going to happen to the women?"

"Well...according to my people, they're a health hazard and should be quarantined. Local immigration wants them deported, via their port of entry, which we believe is Montreal, but authorities up there say it's a local problem."

"And round and round we go…"

"It's such bureaucratic bullshit, Norm. We're talking about kidnapped women forced into the slave trade." Carrie balled her fists on top of the file she held in her lap. She was pissed and I shared her frustration.

"Have you interviewed any of them yet?"

"No, Immigration is still grilling them on their identities and the documents you recovered. They weren't even in their possession. The ID could be fake for all we know."

"That thought already crossed my mind…some of those women were kidnapped at a young age and probably didn't have any documentation…especially if they were smuggled into the country."

"All I can say is that it's a mess, Norm. The good news is that Immigration has nowhere to keep the women overnight so my office secured rooms for them at the Rest Here Inn. We have to keep them quarantined until a legitimate doctor examines them. I'm not sure of the security arrangements yet…maybe you'll be able to talk to your girl there."

My phone rang. It was Roxanne.

Seventy-Five

Long Day

Checking the clock on my phone when I answered Roxanne's call, I realized there was no way to make it to Colchester and get my mother to the cancer clinic for her appointment. My informant was calmer than she had been lately and I wondered if she was high. I quickly gave her the Coles Notes version of the day's events thus far, and told her I'd have to get back to her later.

Mom wasn't upset when I called. Beside myself, she was the easiest going and most laid-back person I knew. She said there was a volunteer driver living near her, and he could probably give her a ride there and back. I felt guilty, but in truth, I had no idea when my day would end and what time I'd be going home.

I left Carrie at the Immigration office and went back to Street Crimes to tackle more of my paperwork. Gamble and I crossed paths in the hallway and I shared my frustrations over the interrogation of the Asian women and their current time in purgatory.

"I hear you, Norm, but it's beyond our control. You might want to think about how you're going to tell Stoker...he's been looking for you, anxious to talk to your Asian source."

"Guess he'll have to wait his turn. Thanks for the head's up."

Bell was banging away on a laptop when I poked my head in the door of the project room. "Hey, Taz, you need anything else from me before I get into my own paperwork?"

"...Can't think of anything right now...did you talk to the Asian peeler yet?"

"No...could be awhile...all the women are being grilled by Immigration. I couldn't get near them. You'd think they're big-time criminals."

Bell scoffed. "They kinda are, Norm, they're prostitutes and illegal immigrants...but I know what you mean." He shrugged and continued typing.

Finding my desk vacant, I piled the other detective's crap in his incoming tray. To get comfortable, I put my coat over the back of my chair and dumped my gun and badge in the top drawer. The message light on my desk phone flashed so I checked the calls to see if there was anything important.

One message was from an ex-Mountie I worked with in the Drug Squad. Disenchanted with the RCMP, he joined the Quebec Provincial Police, and they stationed him closer to home, in Montreal. He was a straight shooter I knew could be trusted. I asked him to track down a doorman named Big Mike.

From the information we obtained on the Montreal end of our investigation, I provided him with the names of three strip clubs and Roxanne's description of Chen's male confidant. Surprisingly, my man came up with the name Michael Fortier. He verified his place of employment and description via his record card and a conviction for assault. Repaying an old favor to me, my friend used his commercial crime connections to locate Fortier's bank and a savings account in his name.

There were no withdrawals...only regular deposits and accrued interest amounting to $37,596. According to my source, it was a joint account with a female by the name of Chen Shen, but no accompanying ID or signature. My ex-Mountie turned QPP pal said the favor put us even. I had to agree; it was more than a fair trade for the time I set him up with a barmaid I knew at a local watering hole. Having Big Mike's real name, address, and phone number, made me feel even more anxious to talk to Chen. I was sure she was more than ready to hear some good news.

As if on cue, Carrie Smith called and said she was buying if I wanted to meet her for a coffee at Tunnel Bar-B-Que. It was right across the street from the Immigration office.

I glanced up at the clock and couldn't believe what time it was.

"You know I don't drink coffee, but since you're buying, I'm sure I can find something to eat there."

"You make twice what I do, mister, how about we share..."

"I like sharing."

"You're bad."

"I know I am. See you there."

The TBQ restaurant was in business before I was born; an internationally famous downtown Windsor landmark. Although it had seen many renovations over the years, the worn out booths still added to the cozy atmosphere. Carrie waved from her seat, when I walked in the door. Noticeably weary from the long day, she was still quite desirable to me. My mind raced, thinking how I wanted to tell her how good she looked. I was dying to get naked with her, but I managed to keep the carnal thoughts to myself.

We talked about the investigation instead. She told me Canadian Immigration was almost done with the women. They waited for some important decisions from the Chinese government. According to Carrie, the Health Department would take over in the morning, conducting their own interviews and medical exams in the privacy of the women's hotel rooms. If I dropped by then, she could probably arrange for me to meet with Chen.

I stared between bites, admiring the contours of her lips, her smooth jawline, and long silky neck, only interrupted by a single mole near her right clavicle. A clingy sweater perfectly outlined her small but adequate breasts. The table prevented my gaze from going any further south, but memory served me well in that area. Washing down the last bite of my burger with water, I sat back and sighed. Carrie followed my gaze.

"Go ahead and ask what you're thinking, Norm, but you're not going to like my answer."

"No? You and I?"

"It's not that I haven't thought about it…I've always liked you. I remember flirting when we met but I found out you were married. I was just getting out of an abusive relationship at that time. After a lot of soul-searching, I confided in a girlfriend who went through the same thing. We became close." She cracked a shy smile. "Very close."

Taken aback by her comment, I sucked my breath in before speaking.

"Let me finish, Norm. I think you're a great guy…and if I wasn't with Sherry and wanted to be with another man, you'd be on the top of my list."

Not one to be embarrassed easily, I still felt my cheeks flush.

"I'm sorry...I should have said something before, but the timing never seemed right."

"Huh. Well, I'd be lying if I said I wasn't disappointed. Guess I'm not the detective I thought I was."

"Don't feel bad...very few people know. I'm very private about my personal life. I hope we can still be friends...and we can still flirt. I like the attention."

"I love teasing you. In case you do get the urge to switch teams again..."

She reached across the table and grasped my hands. "You're a sweet man, Norm Strom. Your wife's crazy for giving up on you...her loss."

I smiled, and for some silly reason, winked. My phone rang.

"My turn to be saved by the bell. It's Roxanne...I was supposed to call her back to update her. Before I talk to her, do you think I could bring her along in the morning? I think Chen would be more at ease and forthcoming if she sees a familiar face."

"I don't see why not...my boss probably wouldn't agree...but what he doesn't know won't hurt him. I'll make it happen."

"Cool. I'm gonna take off and call Roxanne back on my way home."

I grabbed the check off the table and headed for the cash register.

"I was gonna pay half..."

"See you in the morning...I'll call you first."

Seventy-Six

What's Next

It was a struggle to get up the next morning. Four or five hours of sleep wasn't enough, and a problem for me. Late nights and early mornings were taking their toll on my mind and body. I managed to sneak into the hospital after hours, and thanks to a badge courtesy by the ICU, visited my father. Dad said he was fine, good for another ten years or at least sixty thousand miles.

Roxanne wasn't happy I waited so long to return her call. I spoke with her on the way home. I noted she slurred and dragged her words, and assumed she was either drunk or high. It was another reminder no matter how good she looked, I needed to keep it in my pants and steer clear. I gave her a quick recap of my day.

She asked about Rick, Maurice, and the Doctor. I'd already told her earlier. To keep from repeating myself, I said I was losing my phone signal in the county and quickly asked if she wanted to see Chen in the morning. Her answer was yes, but she became long-winded and I told her to meet me at Timmies near the tunnel at 10am. I ended the call.

Brian Gamble waved me into his office as soon as I walked in the door.

"Your father had a heart attack. What the fuck are you doing here? You should be with your family." He caught the puzzled expression on my face. "Tina told me...you remember my girlfriend...the nurse? She saw you leaving the ICU last night."

"He's fine...a double bypass and a valve job. Five siblings, three steps and their spouses, and my stepmother...we have to line up to see him one at a time. I went last night so I could chat up our Asian dancer today and try to put this thing to bed."

"The way you look, bed would be a good place for you. Hey, Shorty's wife is Chinese...maybe he could interview her."

I gave him my best Dirty Harry scowl.

"Your right, forget I mentioned it. He has a hard enough time speaking English."

"No problem, boss, I've got it. Carrie's people are taking a run at the women this morning and she's gonna get me in with Chen. I'm bringing Roxanne along to put her at ease."

"Gotta admit...your CI did okay for us...she definitely earned her money."

"And I'm sure she'll remind me of that. Oh, speaking of money...I found Chen's doorman friend in Montreal. He has a bank account in his and our dancer's name...she's tucked away over thirty-seven grand."

Gamble dropped his pen on the desk.

"Holy shit...maybe you should date her, Norm."

"You're a funny guy. But I do need to get laid...I put it out there with Carrie last night but it turns out she's seeing someone."

"Lucky guy."

I chuckled. "Not quite."

Gamble looked confused, and that's how I left him.

Roxanne sat at a table, coffee in hand, when I walked into Tim Hortons. I went to the counter and ordered drinks and goodies for Carrie and Chen. Nodding toward the door, Roxanne followed me and we walked the short block to the Hotel. It was a mild day for the time of year and the sunshine felt good on my face. Quieter than usual, I assumed Roxanne was hungover. Her gaze was intense and I asked if everything was all right.

"Lots on my mind...Chen...the job I've just lost...and no more money from you."

I paused. I hadn't considered the fallout for someone like her.

"Sorry...try not to sweat it too much. Let's see what comes of all this first, and then see where you stand."

We took a seat in the hotel lobby and I called Carrie's number. While waiting, I sipped on my diet pop and thought about Roxanne. She was different from my other informants. A decent human being who was dealt a shitty hand in life. I had made it worse. That wasn't my intention.

Carrie popped out of the elevator, appearing a bit more frazzled than usual. "Morning...follow me. I put Chen last on the list for our interview, so we have enough time to talk to her alone."

We stepped out onto the third floor. There were suits posted at each end of the hall, Immigration guys I assumed. Chen answered the door and almost melted on the spot when she saw Roxanne. The two women embraced, and I gently nudged them into the room for privacy. I put out the coffee and baked goods on the table while the two friends caught up. Roxanne attempted to introduce Carrie and me, but Chen said she knew who we were.

She held Roxanne's hand and pulled her down to sit beside her on the edge of the bed. Eyeing me point blank, she asked, "What happens next?"

Carrie and I took turns predicting the sequence of events ahead for all the Asian women. The concern on Chen's face never left.

"The border people want proof of my real identity...the stuff you found for all of us has our pictures with different names. They say China doesn't know who we are, and doesn't want us back. Is that true?"

I wasn't sure what to say, and Carrie answered while I gave it some thought. Something Bell said about the doctor's files...how he had his own scam going with fake patients. Maybe the club was doing the same thing, claiming salaries for fake employees. The whole investigation was like a big bowl of spaghetti, and we had to pull on one piece at a time to unravel it.

It was obvious Chen was losing all hope. I told her about contacting Big Mike. Her money was still safe in the bank. Her dark brown eyes grew bigger and she offered me the closest thing to a smile she could muster.

"You've saved a lot of money, Chen, enough to start a new life no matter where you end up. I motioned to the other two women. The three of us are looking out for your best interest. You trust Roxanne and I'm asking you to trust Carrie and me. We'll do everything we can."

I saw her eyeing up the blueberry muffins on the table.

"Help yourself, Chen."

Seventy-Seven

End of a New Beginning

Gamble, Bell, Stoker, and I, spent the next week in meetings and on the phone arguing with officials from Health Canada, Canada Immigration, the Chinese Consulate, CSIS, RCMP, and the Montreal Police. It was as if we poked a giant Grizzly bear, who wasn't ready to emerge from hibernation.

We threw insults and blame at each other like rotten produce. Thankfully, our local action was just enough of a kick in the ass to motive the involved agencies. Police and the Port Authority in Montreal were able to intercept a cargo container from Hong Kong, with a new load of smuggled women.

Shipping manifests had triad written all over them, but the maze of shell companies they controlled created months of work for authorities. The ship itself belonged to a numbered company thought to belong to the same Mr. Wong who Chen worked for, but that would probably never be proven.

Trying to unravel the crime organization and all those involved was like playing a game of Snakes & Ladders. Whenever investigators climbed to another rank in the organization, they found traps and false doors leading them back to where they started. The strip bars and prostitution ring were at the bottom of the triad's business model.

The Asian women rounded up in Windsor remained in limbo at the hotel for more than a week, while the Canadian and Chinese governments argued over where they belonged. Our officials deemed them illegals and wanted them deported. Their home country considered them criminals with unproven identities and didn't want them back.

Eventually, the women received refugee status and told they needed to apply for special visas to get back into their own country. With mixed feelings amongst them, they dispersed in different directions. Their health problems were a great concern but Carrie Smith played a big part in helping the women clear those hurdles.

Chen Shen told me enough about her life and hardships I could write a book. I was able to put her and Big Mike together on the phone. They talked about logistics and returning her hard-earned money. He told her he was looking for other work. They shut down the Montreal clubs temporarily and he had enough of the business.

Roxanne and Chen promised to stay in touch. I doubted it would happen, but hoped they proved me wrong. As with all confidential informants and agents, Roxanne received no official accolades, but she did receive a bonus on top of the small salary she earned.

Using the closure of T & A as an excuse to look for other work, Roxanne asked her other employer if he knew of any job opportunities. The sub shop owner had a cousin who ran six stores in London. He offered her an apartment there above one of the shops, where she could live and still handle the Windsor locations remotely.

I didn't get a chance to say goodbye personally, she called me from the highway on her way out of town. Roxanne said it was easier that way...to just leave her old life behind, and start over.

I have no idea what happened to Maurice and the mysterious copy of the club's books. Stoker thought the Triad disappeared him. They charged Rick with conspiracy in regards to human trafficking, drug possession, and keeping a common bawdy house (prostitution). Fraud charges were impossible to prove. After spending only one night in jail, he was released on bail. Bell tried to have his liquor license suspended but was told it couldn't happen until he was convicted of a crime.

The Doctor from the clinic, Yin, charged with multiple counts of billing fraud, had his medical license suspended for a year, pending the outcome of his criminal trial.

Carrie Smith, recognized for her efforts, received a promotion to a supervisory job within the Health Department. With our career paths going in separate directions, I never had the pleasure of seeing her again. I still think of her from time to time, wondering what if.

Seventy-Eight

A Couple Months Later...

After wrapping up the China Syndrome, I took a well-deserved vacation. My wife and I talked about reconciling, and since we travelled well together, we set off to explore Costa Rica. It didn't take long to figure out I still loved the woman, but too much had changed and I realized we could no longer live together, for better or worse.

The day I returned home, my Superintendent and old car partner called me. I was transferred to Fraud. It didn't matter I was happy in Street Crimes or I did a good job there. It was their way of doing things; shuffling people around even if it meant forcing square pegs into round holes. For those of us who weren't the chosen few, we had no choice.

After cleaning out my desk, I stopped to see Brian Gamble in his office. Kevin Bell was in there with him, and they both said they were sorry to see me go. Tongue in cheek, I suggested it was time to move on since we cleaned up all street crime. Bell told me Rick re-opened T & A with a few of his old regulars and a new crew of Romanian immigrant women.

Fraud had always been a place for dead weight. When I joined the unit, they transferred out the dead weight or forced them into retirement. Arson fell under the Fraud umbrella. That was the real job I wanted, but they gave it to a guy junior to me, with no investigative experience. Not only did my new job suck, but I had to trade in my jeans and tee shirt for business attire.

I did some dating to get on with my life. I put in my time at the new job, chipping away at the two-year backlog of fraud cases. Then one day my old informant, Ham, called. He was working on his second kid and looking for extra cash. I told him I was now in Fraud and he asked if I was interested in a guy making credit cards.

Epilogue

The young woman I knew as Chen Shen eventually made it back to China, and visited her old neighborhood in Shanghai. She thought the taxi driver had dropped her off in the wrong location when she got out of the car. Her house and the block where it sat was now a large condominium complex with hundreds of units. Nothing was recognizable.

She yelled for the taxi to wait and had him drive her around the neighborhood. The only building recognizable was where her mother worked as a seamstress. The dress shop was long gone and a second floor added on to the structure. There was a sign in the window that said, 'For Rent'.

The waterfront had changed too. Towering commercial buildings replaced the fairgrounds. The river was cleaner than she remembered, and the city too. *Progress*...Chen thought. Her next stop was City Hall, where she tried to find out what happened to her family. There was no record of her father, but that didn't surprise her.

It was her mother's death certificate that brought on tears she thought were long suppressed. She was about to return the document, when she caught another name at the bottom. The sole surviving family member was listed as Corporal Guang Shen...her brother. A couple days later, she located the military base where he was stationed. He refused to see her.

Chen was devastated. According to the desk clerk Corporal Shen said he was an only child, and didn't have a sister. She persisted and asked to speak with his commanding officer. About an hour later, a small man with rows of shiny medals covering half his chest, showed up.

The officer glared at Chen as if she was an old enemy. He was abrupt and told her that his men were not allowed to fraternize with whores. She opened her mouth to speak but he pointed to the door and told her to get out.

Chen wandered the strange city for days, wondering if she should bother to stay. Walking the streets in her old neighborhood, reminiscing, she stopped in at a little store dwarfed by the huge buildings around it. She struck up a conversation with the aged woman behind the counter and talked about how things had changed in the city.

When asked if she was from the area, Chen mentioned where she lived and how her mother was a seamstress, and had worked down the street. The old woman stared at Chen for a few seconds and said she knew her mother. She heard her husband disappeared and the son joined the army. The clerk's eyes grew wide as she recalled how the mother thought her daughter, kidnapped as a child, was dead.

Wondering if Shanghai was where she belonged, Chen made her way back to the vacant storefront she had seen for rent. She thought maybe a dress shop, Chen had no other talents that would help her in the business world. She called the number on the sign and a man came down from the apartment above.

He said a gym had previously occupied the main floor and he was renovating the apartment upstairs. The man said to take a look around, that he had to get back to a project he was working on up top. Chen walked around the room, then checked in back, where there was a small office and bathroom. She returned to the empty space up front and stopped to look at the huge mirror, where she thought the sewing machines may have been.

She twisted her neck to get the kinks out, and stretched her calves by standing on her tiptoes. Chen moved the iPod headphones around her neck, to her ears. Swaying her hips to the music, she flipped through the playlist for something more upbeat. The music was familiar and she found her rhythm. The dancer peeled her coat off and flung it to the side.

She felt the beat and turned up the volume. Her hair broke loose when she snapped her head from side to side. Chen flipped it back over her shoulders. Watching her every move in the mirror, Tinkerbell pranced to the beat, perfectly in tune with the music. She held no recollection of her childhood, but vivid memories of being on stage.

Closing her eyes and remembering, she belted out the lyrics to Private Dancer. Her moves came as easily as the memorized words. Chen felt energized. Life had almost bested her, but she survived and the future was hers to explore. Her toe snagged a loose floor tile and she opened her eyes. A reflection in the mirror showed someone standing behind her.

A man with hungry eyes and an anxious lower lip...the landlord.

The End

About the Author

Edmond Gagnon grew up in Windsor Ontario, in Canada. He joined the Windsor Police Department in 1977, a month before his nineteenth birthday. After almost two years as a police cadet, Ed was promoted to Constable and walked a beat in downtown Windsor. He spent the next thirteen years in uniform working the street.

From there, he transferred to plain clothes where he worked in narcotics, morality, property crimes, fraud, and arson. He was promoted to Sergeant and later, Detective. During that time, Ed investigated everything from theft and burglary to arson and murder. He retired with a total of thirty-one years and four months service.

Within weeks of retirement, Ed took to travelling the world, visiting countries in Southeast Asia and South America as well as riding his motorcycle all over Canada and the United States. He kept in touch with family and friends through email, sending them snippets and stories of his adventures.

The recipients of his musings suggested he write a book about his travels and Ed complied by putting together a collection of short stories in his first book, *A Casual Traveler*.

The book was a success. Bitten by the writing bug, Ed decided to share some of his police stories.

He created the Norm Strom Crime Series, based on events and people he encountered during his years in law enforcement. In that series, Ed wrote and self-published *Rat*, *Bloody Friday*, *Torch*, *Finding Hope*, *Border City Chronicles*, and *Moon Mask*. He joined fellow authors Christian Laforet and Ben Van Dongen and put together a crime anthology, *All These Crooked Streets*.

Edmond Gagnon continues to write, adding *Trafficking Chen* to his Norm Strom novels and the spin-off series: the Abigail Brown Crime Series. He also wrote a science fiction thriller called, *Four*. Ed still travels frequently and resides in Windsor, with his wife, Cathryn.

You can see all of Edmond Gagnon's books and more at:
www.edmondgagnon.com